DANGER IN MONTANA

BROTHERHOOD PROTECTORS WORLD

KD MICHAELS

Twisted Page Press LLC

BROTHERHOOD PROTECTORS

ORIGINAL SERIES BY ELLE
JAMES

Brotherhood Protectors Series
Montana SEAL (#1)
Bride Protector SEAL (#2)
Montana D-Force (#3)
Cowboy D-Force (#4)
Montana Ranger (#5)
Montana Dog Soldier (#6)
Montana SEAL Daddy (#7)
Montana Ranger's Wedding Vow (#8)
Montana SEAL Undercover Daddy (#9)
Cape Cod SEAL Rescue (#10)
Montana SEAL Friendly Fire (#11)
Montana SEAL's Mail-Order Bride (#12)
Montana Rescue (Sleeper SEAL)
Hot SEAL Salty Dog (SEALs in Paradise)
Brotherhood Protectors Vol 1

CHAPTER 1

"PATTERSON" Hank 'Montana' Patterson answered as he picked up his cell phone.

"Hey Montana." The voice on the other end said quietly.

"Big Bird?" Hank asked in surprise, alerting his brother-in-law and former team member Axel 'Swede' Svenson across the room.

"Yeah, it's me. How ya been, Montana?" Big Bird asked.

"Doing good man. Sadie and I have a little girl now, her name is Emma. The business is booming. Still got a place for you when you're ready to hang up the pin." Hank told his former teammate with a laugh.

Big Bird laughed on the other end of the

line. "Montana, you know more than anyone we never stop being SEALs. That pin never gets hung up."

"True, true. So, what brings you to call me out of the blue here, Birdman." Hank asked, cutting to the chase.

"Always to the point." Big Bird laughed. "Well, I wasn't sure if you were aware that Jughead died yesterday."

"Aw hell, no I didn't. What happened?" Hank asked on a heavy sigh.

"His vehicle went over a cliff in Colorado. He was heading home to his moms for a few days after a bad mission. He was having a hard time with Shepard's death and just couldn't get his head back into the game. The big man gave him a couple of days RnR and told him to get his head out of his ass or he was off the teams." Big Bird informed Hank.

"Wait, Shepard is gone too?" Hank asked, shocked.

"Yeah, he was killed coming out of a gas station. Police say robbery gone bad." Big Bird answered in surprise. "I thought you knew about Shepard."

"No, I didn't. Shit, no wonder Jughead had a hard time with the news, they were pretty close. I didn't hear about Shepard, damn it.

When's the funeral for Jug?" Hank asked, grabbing pen and paper.

"It's this Saturday, in Colorado. His mother is trying to hold off as much as she can so some of the teams can come in for it." Big Bird explained.

"Saturday is four days away. I will make it. Swede says he's coming too." Hank said, after Swede nodded and pointed at himself.

"Swede is there too?" Big Bird asked surprised.

"Yeah, the lugnut is here with me. He married my sister, Allie. Plus, he helped me get the Brotherhood Protectors off the ground and running." Hank said with a smile.

"Awesome, can't wait to see you both. See you on Saturday. Wish it was on better circumstances." Big Bird said before hanging up.

"So, do we. See you in a few days, Big Bird." Hank replied as he hung up his cell.

"What the hell was that all about?" Swede asked Hank.

Hank relayed all that Big Bird told him about Jughead and Shepard's death. "Something just doesn't sit right with me about their deaths." Hank finished.

"You too?" Swede asked, leaning forward.

"Shepard was the best at being alert in his surroundings. He had better situation awareness than any of us on the teams. He would have figured out a way out of anything before the rest of us could have. Jughead was the best damn driver in the Special Forces community than anyone else I know. I don't know how many times he got us out of sticky situations with his damn driving." Hank answered, placing his hands on his head.

"Damn right, none of this is making any sense. Let's see what happens at the funeral. Maybe use the others as a sounding board. They may know something we don't at this point." Swede suggested.

"Sounds good to me. Let me go let Sadie know that we're going to have to go out of town for a few days. You go and spend some time with Allie and let her know that you're going with me to Colorado. We'll head out in the morning, fly up to Denver and drive the rest of the way to his mom's place, see if she needs any help with anything." Hank said, standing up and walking around his desk.

The next morning Hank and Swede flew from Bozeman, Montana to Denver Colorado, then drove to Jughead's family home. Saturday dawned wet and dreary, as if the heavens cried along with friends and family for Jughead. Several former and current team members gave funny stories, family talked about his younger years. Everyone hugged his mother and sister.

CHAPTER 2

SADIE PATTERSON DROVE along the familiar road towards home after spending the day in Bozeman with her year-old daughter, Emma. Sadie's husband, Hank was due back from Colorado later today. She knew Hank was feeling the loss from Jughead's death. He had a couple of meetings lined up for tomorrow to hire some more people for his personal protection business. Hank started Brother-hood Protectors after he was medically released from the Navy SEALs due to an injury on a mission.

Sadie loved that Brotherhood offered a place for former military, especially former Special Forces like Hank. Sadie knew from firsthand experience with her husband that the men and women in uniform had a hard time transitioning from military life to civilian life. Transitioning to civilian life after so many years of having to be on their toes, looking over their shoulders, dealing with people who wouldn't think twice about taking them out, and constantly having to be alert, even when they were asleep, took its toll on them.

Members of the Brotherhood Protectors were able to continue to protect innocent people, as well as still feel like they were serving their country, while adjusting to their new life. It was a huge adjustment for everyone involved, yet everyone that Hank hired, adjusted very well. It was a huge asset, mentally, physically and emotionally for everyone in the business. Many wound up meeting their special someone while working for Hank. Her best friend, Gypsy Monroe, came to mind in that train of thought.

Sadie listened to her daughter in the backseat babbling, making her smile. She loved hearing her daughter's laughter and baby talk. It always made her heart happy. Emma was the light of her, and Hank's lives. Sadie would have no problems giving up the bright lights of Hollywood to be a full-time mom to her little girl or any other children she and Hank had in the future.

Looking back towards the road, Sadie suddenly slammed on the brakes, skidding to the side of the road, when she saw a dead deer in the middle of the road. Who would hit a deer and then just leave it in the middle of the road like that? Checking to make sure Emma was okay, Sadie picked up her cell phone, getting ready to call one of Hank's men for assistance when chaos erupted all around her.

An off-road vehicle came out of the fields on her left, horn blaring, while shouting at Sadie to put her hands in the air. The driver held a gun outside of their window at her while the passenger doors, both front and the backseat, and the back door in the driver side opened with three men jumping out of the vehicle with weapons pointed at her.

"Get your fucking hands in the air and don't move, bitch. I will shoot you where you stand, leaving your carcass for the buzzards to feast on." Bad guy one shouted at Sadie.

"Please, don't hurt me. My purse is in the

car, take whatever you want, just let me get my daughter out of the car and you can even take the car." Sadie pleaded, her eyes begging to get to Emma.

"I don't give a shit about your purse or your fucking car. I'm taking the brat with me." Bad guy one stated, in a deep growly voice.

"*NO!* Anything but that! Please, you can't take my daughter from me." Sadie begged, trying to get to her daughter before they did.

Just as Sadie moved, several shots were fired, one hitting the ground near her, gravel and dirt spraying up towards her. One bullet hitting the driver side window, shattering it on impact, causing glass to fly out and hit Sadie's face and arms. Another bullet hit the front driver tire, deflating it completely. "I told you not to fucking move, bitch! Next time, I will make sure your husband finds your mangled body on the side of the road instead of you having the luxury of calling him once we're gone." Bad guy one shouted at Sadie as he advanced on her.

"Please, you can't take my daughter!" Sadie begged again, as bad guy two grabbed a screaming Emma out of her car seat.

"Don't forget the diaper bag, dumbass." Bad guy one yelled to his partner. "You, don't let her out of your sight." He informed bad guy three.

"Got it, let's get the hell out of here before someone comes along and sees everything." Bad guy two shouts to the others.

Bad guy one looks over at Sadie with an evil grin, walking up to her, he smacks her hard across the face before he knocks her out with the butt of his gun. Looking down at her body, he grabs his crotch, "You're lucky I don't have more time to play with you." Bad guy one then runs to catch up with his friends at the vehicle he jumped out of. He yells at the driver to haul ass.

Slowly waking up next to her car, Sadie reaches for her phone and dials Hank's number frantically. "Hank, they kidnapped Emma."

"Are you okay? Who took Emma?" Hank asked, worried as he signaled Swede, standing up and heading out of the hotel door.

"I'm okay, my head hurts a little from where they hit me, but Hank, I'm scared for Emma. She was screaming and crying for me and they just took her away. Please, I need you home to help find her. Don't let them hurt my baby." Sadie cried into the phone.

"I'm on my way to the airport now, sweetie. We will find her and bring her home. Don't worry okay? Everything will be fine." Hank said into the phone, trying hard to hide his anger.

"Hurry Hank" Sadie pleaded into the phone.

Hank and Swede jumped into their rented SUV, gunning it to the airstrip where this private plane was gassed up and waiting for them. On the drive to the airstrip, Hank called the Sheriff to give him the heads up of what happened to his wife and daughter. After hanging up with him, Hank then called his team to get to his wife and assess the situation.

Thirty-five minutes after hanging up with his boss, Ranger 'Lone' Logan pulled his SUV to a complete stop before jumping out. Running up to Sadie, he pulled her into his arms and hugged her while she sobbed into his shoulders. "We'll find her, Mrs. Patterson, I promise. The team won't rest until we find her." Lone whispered into Sadie's hair.

Lone turned to his teammates and nodded

to them. Travis 'Wildcard' Carriglitto walked up to them and gently pulled Sadie out of Lone's arms and helped escort her to another teammate to watch over her. "Stick with Mrs. Patterson. Lone and I are going to check around. You and you..." Wildcard said, pointing to two other teammates. "Check Mrs. Patterson's vehicle and the roadway. See if you can find out how that damn deer was killed and if it was recently."

After giving orders to several other teammates, Wildcard walked back over to Lone. "What do we do now? You know the people and the area here like the back of your hand."

"Maybe so, Card, but you're one of the best trackers I've ever seen. It's almost spooky how supernatural your skills are. We need to get the boss's daughter back, yesterday."

"We'll find her, Lone. Come hell or high water, we will find that little girl and have her back in her mother's arms. Sooner rather than later." Wildcard told his friend, as they walked towards where the deer was laying.

Lone, Wildcard and three other teammates canvased the area for hours. The men were getting frustrated with each hour that passed and no signs of who ambushed Sadie or where they went.

"They definitely had an all-terrain vehicle. But the tire treads look odd." Lone mentioned to Wildcard as they were looking at the impressions in the mud.

"Lone, that's not tire treads, that's from chains. These sons of bitches put chains around their tires to either hide their treads or to get better traction for their vehicle." Wildcard pointed out, squatting down to look at the tracks better.

"But why? There's no snow on the ground. Hell, it's only the end of summer. Doesn't make any damn sense to have chains on your tires in this weather." Lone answered, baffled.

"Actually, it tells us a lot. Did Jones get anything else out of Mrs. Patterson? Was she able to describe the vehicle at all?"

"Not much. He said the way she described the vehicle, it's similar to every other truck around here. The truck was dark, gun rack in the back window, and semi beat up with mud caked on it. It was hard for her to really tell the color. Plus, it had some hay in the bed of the truck. That was all she could recall right now." Harris relayed to the men.

"If the truck had a lift kit added on to it, they may have used the chains to hide their treads. Lift kits require specialized tires.

Specialized tire dealers keep a record of those sales for inventory." Wildcard responded, absentmindedly looking around the tracks.

"Son of a bitch!" Lone and Harris said together.

CHAPTER 3

"KAI, ARE YOU OKAY?" Laura 'Red' Pratt asked her co-worker.

"I'm good." Detective Kaileigh Harlin answered quickly.

"No, you're not. Kai, take some vacation time, get your head back into the game. There is no shame in admitting something is wrong. Delta Squad took a hard hit on this case. Losing a teammate, in this case two, as well as a few of the victims of human trafficking is even worse. Your team busted ass to find those girls. And you got them." Pratt said firmly, yet softly.

"I know that, Red. But, damn it, we should have been prepared. We've trained with you guys all the time, you guys are the best..." Kaileigh said.

"But we aren't perfect, Kai. We've been hit, beaten and out-smarted numerous times. We can only thank God it wasn't our time. We learn from our mistakes. We adapt, we train harder than the day before so we can keep on kicking ass." Pratt said, interrupting Kaileigh.

"How do you deal with this, Red? How does it not get to you? Hell, I've done ten years in the Army, assigned to Spec Ops teams, I've lost friends and dealt with the hell I've seen there." Kaileigh admitted with a heavy sigh.

"Going to the gun range. For the longest time, it was looking at Cody and realizing that I'm doing this for him, now it's for all three of my kids, especially my daughter. But, most of all Kai, I do it for those we have rescued, those who are now living their lives back in society making something of themselves. That is what helps me get past the anger and the pain." Pratt said, looking out of their squad room window.

"That, and all the monkey sex she has with squidward." Lindsey 'Ice' Raso said as she walked into the squad room.

"Monkey sex?" Kaileigh asked on a laugh and cough.

"Ignore her ass. She's just jealous." Pratt responded, rolling her eyes.

"Whatever ho! Yes, Kai, she has hot, sweaty monkey sex. He's a squid, well a hot squid. If your ass tells him I said that, I'll deny it, then beat your ass." Raso said, with a glare towards Pratt.

"Well, she's right, he's hot. Does he have any single brothers?" Kaileigh asked, with a hopeful glance at Pratt.

"Several of them!" Pratt said with a smile. "Although one is sweet on Raso, but she keeps ignoring him. I think she's scared of him melting the ice around her cold, cold heart." Pratt said, batting her eyelashes at Raso.

"Keep dreaming sweet cheeks! Ain't happening captain. Nope, no way, no how!" Raso exclaimed, shaking her head.

Kaileigh laughed and shook her head at the same time. "I don't know Raso. Me thinks you protest a little too much."

"I knew I liked her for a reason." Pratt laughed, clapping her hands towards Kaileigh. "By the way, Icey babe, how's monkey boy?"

"Monkey boy?" Kaileigh asked, looking between the two women confused.

"Bug boy, monkey boy – same thing." Cheryl Diesel answered as she walked into the squad room.

"Okay, now I'm really confused, bug boy? Monkey boy?" Kaileigh admitted to the group.

"Raso's gone on a few dates with a guy in her apartment complex who is an exterminator and has a pet monkey." Pratt said, filling Kaileigh in on the joke.

"Monkey huh? That's what he's calling his dick these days?" Kaileigh asked Raso, straight to the point.

"Fuck you all!" Raso, mumbled, flipping her co-workers off at their laughter.

"Have you even done the nasty with him?" Diesel asked Raso, smirking.

"*NO!*" Raso gagged. "We haven't even kissed."

"Umm, has he even tried?" Kaileigh asked, shocked at the no kissing statement.

"Oh, he's tried, but I've been able to put him off so far." Raso admitted.

"Why put yourself through the dates if it's not going anywhere?" Kaileigh asked Raso, shaking her head.

"Cause she's trying to make a certain Scottish hunk of man jealous enough to react." Diesel responded in a fake Scottish accent, causing Pratt to roll her eyes.

"Whatever trampstamp!" Raso retaliated, causing Kaileigh and Pratt to laugh and go 'ohhh' "You all know that asswipe is a man whore. He bangs anything coming or going. I'd probably wind up catching some kind of STD just from being in the same room as him."

"Yeah, a baby is more like it, as strong as them Scottish swimmers are." Diesel snickered, pointing her thumb towards Pratt.

"Meaning he's probably got several baby momma's by now." Raso quipped.

"Nope, a few have tried to claim they were pregnant, but like Highlander, he was way too careful. He may have been a man whore before, hell even Highlander was a man whore before we met, but I can guarantee if you'd even give Pats half a chance there would be no one, but you." Pratt answered, defending her brother-in-law, with a shit eating grin.

"Pats?" Kaileigh asked amused.

"Yeah, Marcus was born on St. Patrick's Day, so his buddies in the Marine Corps started calling him Pats. He's Scottish, not Irish, but they still call him that. His brothers were amused with the nickname, so it stuck." Pratt explained.

"It should be bats because he's batshit crazy if he thinks I'm fucking him to be another notch on his belt." Raso mumbled to her friends.

"As usual…Diesel, I bet you fifty bucks they will cave and wind up together." Pratt said, ignoring Raso's comment.

"Fuck you, ho!" Raso responded again.

"I'm down for that bet, Red. I got fifty bucks on that scenario too." Diesel agreed, high-fiving Pratt.

"Put me down for fifty bucks as well. I say within the next six months the magic will happen." Kaileigh announced, joining in the friendly banter.

"All three of you are going to hell." Raso growled, causing the other women to laugh harder.

"I'm glad to see you laughing, Detective Harlin." Captain Katherine Irby said to Kaileigh as she walked into the squad room.

"I kind of feel guilty ma'am. Two team-mates are fighting for their lives and two are dead. Yet, I'm standing here talking and laughing." Kaileigh admitted to the group, lowering her head, to look at her feet.

"Pick your head up and look around you Detective. Where are you?" Captain Irby asked sternly.

"In the squad room, ma'am." Kaileigh answered, timidly.

"Who. Are. You. With?" Captain Irby asked, moving around the small group of women.

"Alpha Squad ma'am." Kaileigh answered, confused.

"Who are you with?" Captain Irby asked again, more firmly, standing behind Kaileigh.

"Ma'am?" Kaileigh responded in confusion, afraid to move.

"You are with teammates, Detective, family who will walk through the fires of hell with you. Family, who is there besides you through the bad times, the most horrible times, as well as the good times. These three standing here with you right now, are going through hell with you, grieving the loss of two teammates, as well as worrying about Gaines and Stevens too. We will all mourn Hollowman and Brown with you, but *no* one in this room, or this unit, blames you for smiling or sharing a laugh. If they do, you let me know and I will deal with them person-ally. Do you understand me, Detective Harlin?" Captain Irby demanded, standing in front of Kaileigh, with her hands on her hips.

"Yes, ma'am. Thank you." Kaileigh responded, sheepishly.

"You're never alone Kai. My door is always open. You know that. I know most people think we're only close with Bravo Squad, but we support Delta Squad just as well. Unfortunately, you guys get shackled with Charlie Squad more, but, know this, you and your team are always welcomed to come to us, for anything. As the Captain said, we are family, we are here for you." Pratt said, walking over to Kaileigh, pulling her into a hug.

"Now, Detective Pratt, put me down for fifty on Detective Raso giving in to your brother-in-law, but I say it's going to happen in the next two months." Captain Irby said with a shrug.

"Ugh, not you too, ma'am." Raso groaned, slumping down into her chair, as Pratt, Diesel and Kaileigh laughed and clapped.

"Detective, that man has been persistent, he talks to you more than anyone else on the team, expect for Pratt since she's married to his brother. Hell, if I wasn't happily married, I'd give you a run for your money, going into cougar mode." Captain Irby said with a straight face.

"Oh, gross!" Raso gagged, while the other four women laughed. "Anyway, Kai, seriously, there is nothing wrong with taking a few days to get your bearings back or talking to someone. Everyone on our team has done so, there is no shame. We are human, sweetie, not superwomen or robots." Raso finished up, taking the focus off of herself.

"Thanks, Ice. Maybe you're right. It's been a couple of years since I've gone home." Kaileigh said, forming a plan in her mind.

"Where's home Detective?" Captain Irby asked Kaileigh.

Texas, ma'am." Kaileigh answered. "My family still lives on the family ranch I grew up on."

"Oh, nice, what part?" Raso asked Kaileigh.

"Just outside of San Antonio." Kaileigh responded, dreamily.

"Nice, I've never been to that part of Texas. Did a drive through a while back to Kileen, Texas to see my favorite brother-in-law. Texas is a huge ass state." Pratt said, winking and laughing along with a few others.

"Well, we do say everything is bigger in Texas!" Kaileigh laughed, shaking her head.

"Pratt's ex-husband proved that notion wrong." Diesel joked, shaking her head.

"Well, he did prove he was the biggest asshole in the world." Raso said, nonchalantly, causing everyone to laugh harder.

"Detective Pratt definitely upgraded when she married Lt. MacLeod." Captain Irby agreed, winking at Pratt.

"Detective, when was the last time you went home and saw your family?" Captain Irby asked Kaileigh.

"Four years ma'am, just before I got the call that I was accepted into the HTTF. I've been focused on the team." Kaileigh admitted to the group.

"When was the last time you spoke with them?" Diesel asked in shock.

"I spoke with my sister for a few minutes today." Kaileigh answered quietly.

"Before today?" Captain Irby pushed.

Kaileigh shrugged, "Maybe a couple of months or so."

Captain Irby sighed deeply. "Detective, I'm going to give you two weeks leave."

"Ma'am…" Kaileigh started.

"No, you're not in trouble or on admin leave. I'm giving you the vacation time to go see your family, because Detective, after the funeral, you *will* be raw and need them more than you realize." Captain Irby emphasized.

Kaileigh sighed, "Maybe getting back to my roots is what I need right now. I do kind of miss riding the horses right now."

"There you have it. Let me know your flight plans, I'll take you to the airport." Pratt said, giving Kaileigh a squeeze.

"Yay, I'm going home." Kaileigh said, sarcastically.

CHAPTER 4

HANK PATTERSON LANDED IN BOZEMAN, anxious to get home to his wife and see for himself she was ok. Hank stayed in constant contact with his team as much as possible since his daughter was kidnapped while he'd been away. No one touches his family without facing the consequences. Hanks thoughts kept swaying to his little girl. He prayed she was okay and that whomever had her was taking good care of her. God help them if they harmed his baby girl.

Several hours later, Hank and Swede pulled into the driveway of his home. Hank jumped out of the SUV and ran into the house. "Sadie?"

"Hank?" Sadie yelled out from the living room. "Hank!" Sadie yelled again, as she ran into the foyer, launching herself into his arms.

Hank held on to his wife as if his life depended on it at that moment. "I'm home babe. We'll find Emma, I promise."

"I know you will, Hank." Sadie said, looking into her husband's eyes. "I just hate thinking about what Emma is going through without us."

"Think positive, honey. They are taking care of her." Hank said, trying to not only assure his wife, but himself as well.

"Their lives depend on it." Swede said, his tone fierce, walking into the room, stopping behind Hank.

"What does that mean?" Sadie asked her brother-in-law.

Before Hank or Swede could respond, Wildcard and Lone walked into the door, giving them a slight nod of their head. Hank nodded back to the two men, then nodded towards his office. Swede, Wildcard, and Lone quietly went into the direction of Hank's office.

"Sadie, go back into the living room with Jones. I'm going into the office to talk with

Swede, Wildcard and Lone. I'll be back in a few moments, okay?"

As Sadie nodded, Hank placed a kiss on her forehead and watched her slowly walk aback towards the living room. Hank made eye contact with Jones and both men nodded to each other.

"Better tell me you have something." Hank said as he walked into his office.

"Whoever took Emma definitely knew what they were doing. There were no casings found on the ground. The bullet that hit her car shattered on impact..." Wildcard started to say.

"They shot at my wife?" Hank questioned, low and deep.

"They fired at the car, according to Mrs. Patterson, when she made a step towards the car to grab Emma." Wildcard confirmed.

"These guys knew who they were going after Hank. They left Mrs. Patterson alive for a reason, shot out all four tires, yet left her cell phone alone so she can call for help when they left." Lone told Hank and Swede.

"They didn't want to harm Mrs. Patterson, it was about controlling her to get to your daughter. Jones talked to your wife, she said she hasn't noticed anyone paying extra attention to them..." Wildcard said, trailing off.

"Which means it's someone we know." Swede growled, looking over at Hank.

"Who would be stupid enough to go after my family? We haven't had any threats, verbal or written." Hank said, standing up from his desk with a heavy sigh.

"That you know of...sir." Wildcard said at Hanks glare.

"Hank think about it, Mrs. Patterson was left unharmed, only scared out of her skull. Emma was the only one taken. Everyone in town knows you and Swede were out of town." Lone said, backing up Wildcard. "We live in a small town. It doesn't take much around here to get information. You were the town hero as the football star turned Navy SEAL. She's your high school sweetheart who went on to become Hollywood's sweetheart."

"If it was about Mrs. Patterson, they had a chance to cause her harm or take her, instead..." Wildcard repeated with emphasis.

"As much as I hate it, I have to agree with them Hank." Swede admitted with trepidation.

Hank's desk phone rang, breaking the

silence in his office. "Patterson" Hank answered.

"I see that my message has brought the big man home from the wild blue yonder." The distorted voice replied.

"Where's my daughter?" Hank growled.

"Safe...for now." The voice replied, starkly.

"What do you want?" Hank asked, sitting down, watching Swede text instructions to their tech guy.

"World peace, world domination, endless pussy, to be rich...take your pick. I'm not hard to please really. Guess you could even say... I'm easy." The voice said, with a harsh laugh into the phone.

"So, you ran my wife off the road and kidnapped my daughter for world peace?" Hank asked with a scoff.

The voice laughed, loud and harsh. "Oh, hell no. See, the reason I took your cute spawn is much more. You see, Hank Patterson, your family cost me mine. So, I'm taking yours."

"Who are you?" Hank growled, barely controlling his temper.

"All in good time, Mr. Patterson, all in good time. I'm going to enjoy seeing you scramble to figure out who you destroyed. I'm going to let you wonder if you'll ever see your little girl again. I can tell you this, your daughter is the first of many things I will take from you. I'm nowhere near done with you, Mr. Patterson. Oh, and if you even think of sending the wifey away, I will find her, then send you parts of wife and daughter, body part, by beautiful body part. That is after I've had a little fun with them." The voice said, laughing again, as they hung up in Hank's ear.

"He's a sadistic bastard, that's for damn sure." Wildcard stated, shaking his head.

"Swede, I want you, Lone and Wildcard to go over every case we've had in the last three years. Check letters and emails that we've received that were considered threatening. I'm going to arrange more security for the house and a team for Sadie and Allie. I'm not taking any more chances with my family." Hank ordered his men, as he picked up the phone on his desk again.

"You do know the women are going to revolt right?" Swede asked his brother-in-law.

"They will have to get over that shit. I'm *not* taking any chances after this call." Hank repeated.

"Are you recalling those that are on vacation? We have three on leave, seven off for the next couple of days and several on cases currently." Swede informed Hank.

"The ones on current assignments, leave them on their assignments until further notice. Go ahead and recall the seven who are days off. Leave the three on vacation for now. If it gets worse, then we can recall them." Hank decided, pulling out his team rosters as he dialed numbers. "Get busy."

"Alright boys, daddy has given us our marching orders. Let's get busy and find this asshole." Swede said, saluting Hank, before walking out the door, laughing as Hank flipped Swede the middle finger.

"Hey Swede" Hank called out, holding the phone in his hand.

"Yeah?"

"Would I be overreacting if I brought in Alpha Squad? They would be neutral in the search for Emma. They have fresh eyes, fresh ears, and a fresh perspective all the way around."

"Sir, are you sure that it's a good idea to bring in more people, outsiders, much less, with the threats this guy just made?" Lone asked Hank, concern in his voice.

"Yes! These ladies are meticulous. They are almost as good as some of the Spec Ops I've dealt with. *Almost!*" Hank said, at Wildcard and Lone's questioning look.

"Hank's right. We are all too close to this. We would probably overlook the simplest things because we know everyone in this town. They don't have any ties here, so they can see what we wouldn't." Swede explained, catching on to Hank's train of thought.

"Plus, if it comes down to it, these women will protect Sadie with their lives. They will even guard Emma's life as well, once she's found." Hank claimed, confident in his decision.

"Sadie and Emma will become one of theirs, God help anyone who means them harm, now or in the future." Swede agreed.

"They definitely earned the nickname Rottweilers." Hank chuckled as he started dialing numbers.

"So, we're bringing in a bunch of wildcats to help in the search for Emma." Wildcard stated, amused.

"Card, don't let these women hear you call them wildcats. They will tear into your ass." Swede said with laughter.

"He'd probably like that with some of the

action he's been getting lately." Lone joked, shaking his head.

"Betty Sue wasn't bad the other night." Wildcard joked, causing Lone and Hank to choke on their laughter.

"You played with slutty Betty Sue? Allie can't stand her. Don't let my wife hear you talk about that one." Swede said, backing away, fake gagging as he walked towards Hank.

"Boys, you will see. They are good people. Gypsy Monroe is one of theirs. They rescued her years ago. When Gypsy was here visiting, her past came back to get her, they dropped everything to come and save her. They are dedicated, each one of those women will stop at nothing to get the job done. I trust them with my life and the lives of my family." Hank stated, leaning down onto his desk to show his determination.

"Okay boss man, we are behind you. Whatever you want to do." Lone said, agreeing.

CHAPTER 5

"Riverton County Sheriff's Office, Sgt Brocard speaking, how may I help you?" Sgt. Helen Brocard said, answering her cell phone.

"Hi Brocard, it's Hank Patterson, how are you?"

"Hank! I am doing good. How are you and the family?"

"I wish I could say we were good." Hank said quietly.

"Hank, what's wrong?" Sgt. Brocard asked, sitting up straighter in her chair, alerting the Alpha Squad women. "Hold on, let me put you on speaker for the rest of the team."

"Hi ladies." Hank said, as he took a deep breath. "I wish I was calling for another reason, but I really need your help here in Montana."

"Hank, it's Pratt here, what's going on? Talk to us."

"Sadie was attacked yesterday evening while I was in Colorado for a funeral. The men who attacked her kidnapped Emma."

Gasps and harsh words were heard around the room. "What do you need from us Hank? We will help in anyway we can." Sgt. Brocard responded instantly without hesitation.

"Is Sadie okay, Hank?" Pratt asked, worry in her voice.

"Thank you, yes, she's okay, physically. They didn't harm her, but they scared the living hell out of her. They shot at her, taking out all four tires of the vehicle. Shot at her when she tried to stop them from taking Emma out of the car."

"Well, we know Diesel is going to get to have some fun when we find the sons of bitches." Raso growled.

"That's what I'm counting on. I could really use your help out here."

"How can we help you?" Raso asked, repeating Sgt. Brocard's question.

"I need your help here in Eagle Pass. We

are all too close to everyone here. You guys would be unbiased. We need that badly right now. I need someone without prejudice and knowledge of the people here. Someone not afraid to step on toes to get the job done. I am desperate here ladies. I need your help finding my daughter."

"Let me talk to Captain Irby. Once she approves the trip, we'll be in later tonight or first thing in the morning. We will call you with our flight details." Sgt. Brocard promised, making notes as she spoke with Hank.

"She can call me if she needs verification or has any questions about the situation." Hank said before he hung up.

Sgt. Brocard looked at her team, "Ok everyone, go get your bags packed. Pratt, inform the hubby and make the necessary arrangements you'll need in case he gets called away while we are gone. Everyone be back here in an hour and a half. That will give me time to talk to the Captain and then make the same arrangements with my family."

The team went their separate ways as Sgt. Brocard went in search of the Captain to talk with her about Hank's phone call. Twenty minutes later, the team was sent a text messages informing them that the trip to Eagle Pass, Montana was a go.

"Hello?"

"They brought in outside help to search for the brat." Bad guy two informed the other person.

"How did you find out?" Bad guy one answered, clearly agitated.

"Waitress at the local diner mentioned it, while talking with one of the deputies. She was asking if they had any clues on who took the kid." Bad guy two said, enthusiastically.

"That doesn't mean jackshit." Bad guy one fired back.

"The dumbass deputy was grumbling about how the family brought in a team of chicks from San Diego to hunt for the brat."

"They brought in women from San Diego to hunt for this kid?" Bad guy one repeated, amused.

"Yep. The deputy wasn't happy about it since he called them uneducated big city slickers. Says no such thing as a task force full of women, unless they have professional knee pads to get their position." Bad guy two said, laughing.

"Sounds like our friendly deputy isn't too happy with these turns of events. See if you can befriend our local deputy, to keep up with the hunt for this kid. We wanna stay a few steps ahead of everyone." Bad guy one ordered.

"They ain't never gonna find the brat." Bad guy two said, on a huffy laugh.

"No, and since daddy wants to bring in outsiders, it's time to go to the next phase of our plan." Bad guy one smirked into the phone. "Keep your eyes and ears opened."

"OH FUCK!" Diesel said out loud, looking up from the computer screen to her teammates.

"What's up Diesel?" Pratt asked as she walked into the room with Raso, and Cortez behind her.

"I just got two…shit, now four, notifications on facial recs on the Patterson kid." Diesel explained, as she checked the notifications coming in.

"Where?" Tarilyn 'Taz' Cortez asked her teammate.

"A couple of the human trafficking sites we regularly check. Holy shit, one just popped up on a dark web adoption site and now a dark web organ donation site." Diesel exclaimed, looking at everything.

"Shit, this is not good guys. Whoever this is, he's really going after the Patterson's." Raso groaned.

"Cortez, you have a friend who is a computer wizard we can use right now?" Sgt. Brocard asked, leaning onto the table.

"Yep, I can reach out to Oz. He's one of the best that I know." Cortez said, pulling out her phone as she stepped out of the room.

"This really isn't good. We can't tell Sadie about this. We have no choice but to inform Hank, unfortunately." Pratt sighed.

"Taz, can your friend find the IP location of the person posting the photos on these sites without engaging them?" Sgt. Brocard yelled out to Cortez.

"Hold on." Cortez answered back before speaking into the phone some more.

Ten minutes later, Cortez walked back into the room. "He's going to do some looking into things. I've forwarded a picture of Emma to him. He's running facial rec himself to make sure everything adds up and it's not someone fucking with us."

"How would they know about us already?" Kaitlyn Rameriez asked. "We haven't spoken to anyone here, yet."

"Small town and we've been here before." Pratt responded looking over Diesel's shoulder at the computer screen. "If you'd been paying attention to the people, we'd been getting some heavy stares as we were getting out of the car and checking into the hotel."

"Pratt's right, it's a small town. You sneeze wrong and it's all over town before the end of the day. Everyone knows about Emma's disappearance." York said, confirming Pratt's comment.

"Exactly. Everyone knows about us after we came here for Gypsy to help her out. Hank had to field questions about us for weeks." Raso reminded the team.

"Wouldn't their kidnappers have stood out then?" Rameriez asked, a question the whole team had about the situation.

"According to Hank when I spoke with him a little more before leaving San Diego, Sadie said the kidnappers wore a mask, so she didn't get to see their faces. She was only able to discuss the vehicle and what they wore. She wasn't able to give much of a description since she had been more focused on trying to get to Emma." Sgt. Brocard informed the group, steel in her voice.

"Did Hank's men do a perimeter search where the kidnapping took place?" York asked, making notes.

"Yes, according to him, they didn't find much. They found some tracks, but they were a bust since they used chains on the tires to hide them. They apparently lost them when they hit the grass." Pratt said, with some confusion in her voice.

"What? I know that tone." Raso said.

"Wouldn't the chains still not leave an impression in the grass? I mean wouldn't it dig up some of the grass as well, since there's likely to space between the tire and chains to cause the grass to get caught?"

"Good questions. Let's doing some digging of our own." York said, nodding then looking at their team leader.

"I agree, we need to look at this our way. Then we can coordinate with Hank and his men for further information." Sgt. Brocard said, standing up. "Pratt, I want you and Raso to talk with Sadie. See what information about the kidnappers you can get from her. I want York, Cortez and Diesel to work the scene where the kidnapping went down. Rameriez and I will double check the vehicle and perimeter to make sure what equipment we find belongs to Patterson. Cortez, have your friend keep an eye on those websites and keep us updated."

CHAPTER 6

"LAURA!" Sadie screamed out with a mixture of happiness and sadness.

"Hi, Sadie!" Pratt said, giving her a hug. "Sorry we are getting together under these circumstances.

Sadie sighed as she turned and led the team into the living room. Hank, Lone, Swede and Wildcard stood by the living room windows, conversing until Sadie and the others had walked into the room.

"Hank, Alpha Squad is here." Sadie announced.

The men separated, watching the women walk into the room. Hank and Swede stepped towards the women and smiled.

"Hank" Pratt said, shaking hands with

Hank and Swede. "You remember Raso, York, and our team Sgt., Brocard."

"Ladies, good to see you again. I'm sorry it's under these circumstances!" Hank said, shaking hands with the women.

"Us too. We'd like to talk to both of you and get a feel of the situation…" Pratt started.

"What more do you need? Their daughter was kidnapped, and Hank needs your assistance." Lone asked, irritated about the questions being asked already.

"Stand down Lone. These women are not saying you boys did anything wrong. They are wanting to do their own investigation to get their own opinions." Swede ordered, defending the women.

Sadie, will you be willing to sit down with Detectives Pratt and Raso to go over the event with them?" Sgt. Brocard asked Sadie, ignoring Lone.

"We already told you everything she gave us." Wildcard answered tensely, getting upset along with Lone.

"Are you a woman?" Raso spoke up, defending her Sgt.

"Excuse you?" Wildcard asked confused by the question.

"Women tend to not think about certain

things when giving descriptions to men. But, when talking to another female, they tend to remember more details about their attackers. They don't have to worry about another female judging them as weak." Raso said firmly.

"She knows us, we'd never think of her as weak." Lone said, defending his friend.

"Mrs. Patterson..." York started, ignoring the outbursts.

"Please call me Sadie."

"Okay, Sadie, you told Logan and this other guy that the vehicle was a truck that needed to be badly washed. Did you notice anything beyond that?" Pratt asked, without looking at Sadie.

"Yes, it had a few dents in the door on the passenger side. The front of the truck, the silver part, had some dents in it as well, looked like part of it was missing also. It had those big lights across the top of the truck, extra lights on the silver thing in front of the truck too. Oh, and the tires were bigger than normal tires. Kind of like they had them lifted or something." Sadie said, looking around the room.

"So, the grill of the truck was dented up and had running lights. Did you see what color the truck was?" Pratt asked, still looking at Lone and Wildcard with a smirk.

"Well that was kind of hard to tell. It looked like a dark color, maybe dark blue or black, but it was hard to tell with all the dried-up mud on it. It looked like they purposely put all the mud over it, trying to hide the truck or something." Sadie said, looking over towards Hank.

"Sounds about right. You guys live in a small town. They could have intentionally covered the truck with dirt and mud to hide any distinguishing features about it. Sadie, you said the tires were big, like they went bigger than normal?" Raso asked Sadie, writing down some notes into her book.

"Yes, like those monster truck tires." Sadie answered, looking down at her fingers.

"What about the windows? Were they clear? Tinted? Dirty? Have any stickers anywhere on the truck or the windows?" Pratt asked, looking out the window at Hank's truck.

"I could see through the windshield, but the sides were all dirty with mud too." Sadie answered, cocking her head to the side like she's trying to recall the image of the truck. "I don't think there were any stickers, well, that I could see. I honestly wasn't looking."

"You still did awesome Sadie. You still gave us a lot to work with. Don't worry about the stickers, honestly most don't really think to look for those when they are dealing with chaos." Sgt. Brocard said, rubbing Sadie's shoulder.

"They were definitely trying to cover themselves." York said, looking over at her teammates.

"Mr. Logan, you stated that you and Mr. Cariglitto noticed impressions that supported this, but it also showed that the treads had what appeared chain link marks?" Raso asked the two men.

"We've already come to that conclusion." Wildcard answered, huffy.

Just then, Pratt's phone rang. "Hey Rameriez, what do you have?" After several minutes on the phone, Pratt hung up and looked over at the men. "Sadie, which way did they come in towards your vehicle?"

"Well I was coming home from Bozeman, so I was going south towards the ranch. There's nothing but fields on both sides so they came in at me from the passenger side. Why?"

"Did you boys check the field to the east or only to the west of her vehicle?" Pratt asked Lone and Wildcard.

"The field she saw them come from. We checked a small portion of the opposite side and didn't see anything." Lone shrugged.

"Cortez, Rameriez and Diesel found the exact same tracks coming from the opposite side. Looks like they threw everyone off by coming in on the passenger side and leaving that way. But what they did was circle around through some property. They ran into a dipshit Barney Fife looking deputy who wanted to throw some attitude when the three showed up to look at a fence that was down on a nearby ranch. Looks like they cut through that ranch to get back to the opposite side. The three are following it now." Pratt informed the men.

"How far back?" Wildcard asked, perplexed.

"About a mile back. These guys are smart, which tells me they have training, and that they know the area very well. So, it could be locals. Hank, besides you, Swede and Mr. Logan here, who else from here has military training that knows this area like the back of their hand?" Pratt asked Hank and Swede.

"Not very many. Around here, it's mostly expected for the son to follow in their father's footsteps and take over the ranch to keep it in the family. Usually it's the second or third kid, if they aren't needed on the ranch, which is very rare, that goes into the military. Lone and I did it to piss our parents off." Hank said, running his fingers through his hair.

"Actually, Hank did it to piss his parents off. I was expected to do the four years, like my father did and our grandfather. It just pissed my dad off when I re-enlisted for another 6 years to join the Special Forces." Lone said, laughing at the memory.

"What's so significant about the tires that you mentioned?" Sadie asked in a confused tone, looking between Hank and the three women.

"Well, it's not well known but tires for monster trucks or with lift kits are registered. The truck information is stored with the inventory that is sold. By inventory we mean the kit itself which has its own serial numbers, the number of tires bought as well as size, and any other changes made to the vehicle to make sure everything fits." Raso informed Sadie.

"But it still doesn't tell us who it is." Lone told Raso.

"Actually, it does…" Raso started to say.

"Lone, call me Lone. I feel like you're speaking to my father when you call me Mr. Logan."

"Very well, Lone, it does help us. All we need to do is check out the local shops here, find out who's done a lift kit in the last several years and then go from there." Raso finished.

"We've already done that." Wildcard informed the group. "There's only been two people in the last two years and neither one of them were in town at the time of the kidnapping and both had their vehicles with them in Bozeman. We've already checked out their alibi's."

"Okie dokie, that only confirms our theory that the person who did the kidnapping isn't local. They could have had it done in Bozeman, but more than likely elsewhere." Raso said, glaring at Wildcard.

"Theory? So, you're running off theories? You ladies do realize we have a little girl missing? She doesn't have time for you to test your theories." Wildcard said heatedly.

"Travis, that was uncalled for." Sadie

informed Wildcard clearly upset. "These women are damn good at what they do and would never think of allowing anything more to happen to my daughter. If you're upset that they managed to figure out in a couple of hours, what took you boys two days to figure out, then I'm sorry. But these girls are dang good, and I will not have them disrespected."

"I'm sorry Mrs. Patterson. That's not what I meant. I am upset with myself because I didn't catch the tracks like they did. I apologize to you both." Wildcard said, boyishly.

"Look, we aren't here to step on any toes. Hank calls the shots here. We need to work together. You guys are former military and have skills we don't. We deal with human traffickers for a living and know how men like that think. We have skills in that area that can be useful to you, especially since we can access the dark web faster than you guys probably can right now. We need to work together to get Emma home safe and sound, yesterday." Sgt. Brocard said to the room.

CHAPTER 7

Sgt. Brocard sent Raso to assist with the scene of the kidnapping, Lone and Wildcard insisted on going alone to make sure 'nothing else happened'. Sgt. Brocard, Pratt, and Raso rolled their eyes and agreed, just to keep the peace. Raso told the two men they would have to drive their own vehicle just to be a bitch.

Arriving at the scene, Raso met up with Cortez, Rameriez and Diesel to discuss what was found. Lone and Wildcard followed them to where they saw the change in directions, the spot that may be their big break in finding little Emma.

"Son of a bitch, I didn't see this. How the

hell did you find it?" Wildcard asked, upset about missing the tracks.

"Pure luck, considering we know jack shit about this area." Cortez informed the men.

"Lone, this direction heads towards the Twilight Ranch." Wildcard observed the directions, noticing where the tracks went.

"Wait a minute, did you say the name of the ranch is called 'Twilight'?" Diesel asked, amused.

"Oh God help us!" Cortez mumbled.

"Yes, some head honcho out of Los Angeles bought the old Jameson Ranch a couple of years ago. His son Jasper Culpepper now runs the place." Lone informed the women.

"Well, the son's name is Jasper." Diesel smirked at Cortez.

"Wasn't he the cute vampire that had the southern drawl?" Rameriez asked, looking deep in thought.

"What the hell are you two yammering about now?" Wildcard asked, losing patience with the small talk.

"Twilight is the name of a movie, about vampires that sparkle like diamonds if the sun hits them. Was a vomit inducing series of movies, young teenage love and all that garbage." Cortez informed the men, shuddering.

"Wait a minute, wasn't that the name of the movie with the goofy looking shirts that women would wear to our team get gatherings?" Lone asked, laughing at the memory.

"Everyone knows that Team Jacob was the way to go!" Rameriez said, laughing at Cortez's fake gag.

"Let me know when y'all return to adulthood." Cortez quipped.

"This coming from the twittletwat who watches Vampire Diaries, another tween saga about vampires." Diesel fired back.

"I've never watching vampire diaries, spank you very much. I've always, and still watch, Supernatural." Cortez corrected Diesel with a smirk.

"Oh, yes, I love that show. Dean is so damn dreamy. And his car?! Ugh, I love his car." Raso said with a huge sigh.

"Yes, Lord have mercy, that car was orgasmic." Rameriez sighed dreamily.

"Moving on." Lone said, with a shake of his head. "As I said a little bit ago, the ranch was brought out and is now run by the son, Jasper. It's said the place has state of the art security surrounding it's perimeter." Lone said, informing the group about the ranch.

"Apparently it's not state of the art if Emma's kidnappers went through without detection." Diesel mentioned, reminding the group of why they were gathered around.

"She's right. They had to know something about the Culpepper's security system and how to get around it. We will have to talk to him and have a look at the system itself." Cortez stated, as she looked around.

"Unless he's a part of it." Rameriez said absent mindedly, looking out at her surroundings.

"Shit, they are right. There are three ranches here. Had they gone to the left, they would have run smack dab into the Triple L Ranch. Stay north, they would have gone into Diablo's Ranch. But they went right, which took them to Culpepper's Ranch." Lone said, looking at his surroundings.

"Who owns the Triple L?" Diesel asked the group.

"I do." Lone answered, with a small bite in his tone. It's ran by myself and my sister Lisa."

"Nice! What about Diablo's?" Cortez questioned Lone.

"That's owned by Francisco Diablo. The

ranch has been a part of his family for eight generations now." Lone stated, looking in the direction of Diablo's ranch.

"Frank went to school with Lone. His parents died a year before his did. One of those hometown 'love' deaths." Wildcard informed the four women.

"Hometown love deaths?" Rameriez asked, confused.

"Are you from here too?" Diesel asked Wildcard.

"No ma'am." Wildcard answered, smiling.

"The elder Diablo's married young. Frank Sr went into the Army, met his wife while on TDY and married her against his father's wishes. Sr was twenty and his young bride was sixteen. They had six kids with Jr being the youngest. They were like newlyweds until the day they died. Sr got sick with cancer and she had heart trouble. Apparently, the day he died, the wife died a few minutes after him. They were married for a little over fifty something years before they died." Lone told everyone with a sad smile.

"Yeah, that's small town 'love' right there." Cortez agreed, smiling.

"Okay, so we know they didn't go to the Triple L or the Diablo's. So, we think they know the Culpepper Ranch?" Wildcard asked, getting everyone back on track.

"We can ride out to the Triple L and double check the perimeter. We have a good security system as well. Hank set it up himself when I joined Brotherhood Protection. Everyone that works for Patterson has been with him for years. There are a few new members, but, Hank vets them inside and out. He and Swede go over everything several more times before he makes a decision on hiring them or not." Lone said, shrugging. "As for my ranch hands, everyone that works on the ranch has been there for years, some even started working for my father as teenagers. Diablo's ranch is the same. But I'm sure if we talk to Blakely, he'll join us to double check his perimeter as well." Lone answered.

"Culpepper is new to the area. Are his ranch hands from the previous ranch, or are his people new to the town too?" Raso speculated.

"A couple of the original ranch hands agreed to stay on and help them train the guys that Culpepper brought in from elsewhere." Lone said, shrugging and shaking his head at the loss.

"Have there been any issues with the new

ranch hands in town?" Cortez asked the two men.

"Some bar fights at the local watering hole, but most of the issues were in Bozeman. Fred, the senior foreman at Culpepper's ranch was complaining about a few of the out of towners." Lone answered, looking at Wildcard for confirmation.

"Culpepper's ranch has a high turnover rate for their ranch hands. He refuses to hire local people." Wildcard confirmed. "It's caused some high tension between the locals and the men Culpepper brings in to help out on the ranch."

"Wonder why he refuses to hire any of the locals?" Rameriez questioned in a wondering tone.

"Which can cause tempers to flare. Makes our job both hard, yet easy." Diesel sighed.

"How the hell do you figure that?" Lone asked, confused.

"Easy, because it's not locals, so there won't be resistance from the locals needing to protect one of their own." Cortez responded.

"Hard as hell because we'll have to track them all down and figure out who the hell they are, where they are from and why they may have targeted the Patterson's. Can't be land reasons because the Patterson ranch is thirty minutes away." Raso answered, backing up Diesel and Cortez's thinking.

"So, you ladies are thinking out of towners are who took Emma?" Lone questioned.

"That's what we're leaning towards. But at the same time, they've been here long enough to learn the lay of the land. We can rule out anyone who's been in town a year or less." Rameriez said as she looked around her.

"I agree. These roads, and the land layouts take at least that long to learn how to navigate and know where to avoid." Raso agreed.

"Let's double check the perimeter of the other two ranches, just to be safe, then we can check out Culpepper's. I want Sgt. Brocard with us when we deal with this guy." Cortez decided.

"Thinking of issues?" Wildcard asked Cortez, trying to figure out her train of thought.

"Not sure. I want you two with us as well. We'll talk to Hank and Swede to get their input on Culpepper before we head over there. But where we are concerned, having someone with rank usually helps with rich assholes." Raso answered matter-of-factly.

"Why not have Pratt talk to Culpepper? She's from the rich crowd like he is." Cortez suggested to Raso.

"Do *not* let Pratt know you suggested that shit." Diesel said, backing up with her hands in the air.

"Diesel is right. Just because she was born into a wealthy family doesn't mean shit to her. She hates the rich who think they are God's gift to the world, abusing their power against those less fortunate." Raso informed everyone. "She'd probably wind up crucifying Culpepper if he stepped one foot out of line in the conversation."

"Ah daddy cut her off and forced her to get a real job?" Wildcard said laughing in a lame attempt at a joke.

Diesel walked towards Wildcard with a pissed off look on her face. "Diesel, don't do it." Raso warned her teammate before turning to him. "You know *Wildcard*, for a smart man, you're really a dumbass. Pratt chose to be a cop instead of a jarhead or a congressman's trophy wife. She has more brains in her entire body than you do in your left pinky."

"Pratt's family expected her to be simply a wife who looked the other way while her ex-husband fucked around. If she did say something, he would beat her senseless. He is the son of a California congressman who has his hands in several criminal enterprises. She wanted to work, so she left her marriage to raise her son alone on a cop's salary without her family or ex-husband's assistance. I suggest you do your homework before spouting shit like that." Diesel growled out low

"Shit, I'm sorry guys. You're right, I'm a dumbass. I shouldn't have said that. So, let's go check the perimeter of Triple L and talk to Blakely Jr about Diablo's. Then we can head back to the Patterson ranch and talk with Hank about our theory and go from there." Wildcard responded, cringing as he ran his fingers through his hair.

CHAPTER 8

THREE HOURS LATER, Wildcard, Lone, Cortez, Diesel, Rameriez and Raso pulled into the Patterson Ranch. After walking into the house, they had a quick lunch before having a meeting in Hank's office.

"What did you guys find out?" Hank asked, cutting to the chase.

"They knew where they were at. The location gave them access to three ranches, the Triple L, Diablo's and Twilight." Lone answered his boss.

"Wait a minute? Twilight?" Pratt asked, chuckling.

"Yeah and?" Swede asked sighing over the twilight name, again.

"For the love of God, can we please focus on this case?" Cortez mumbles to her team.

"I agree with Taz, no bullshit talk about team sparkle dick and team wooly mammoth" Pratt says, glaring at Diesel and Raso.

Brocard, Cortez, York and the men choke on their laughter as Raso and Diesel gasp.

"Team sparkle dick?" Raso gasped.

"Jacob was *not* a wooly mammoth you heifer!" Diesel yelled out. "He was a shapeshifter who became a hot as hell big ass wolf!"

"Either way, the movie sucked. Now, as Taz said, let's focus on this case because I for one want Emma home with her parents. I want this asshole who took her to pay. Are you done crying about the wooly mammoth?" Pratt asked Diesel with a daring glance.

"You're right, I'm sorry, Mr. Patterson." Diesel sighed, turning towards the group. "Okay, as Lone said earlier, before he and the others showed up, Cortez, Rameriez and I found some tracks. We followed it out of curiosity because of how weird the tracks looked. It led us to some fences that looked like they were torn down and haven't been repaired. When your two guys and Raso showed up, they informed us that the location was the border of three ranches, but the one it looked like they crossed into was the Twilight one."

"You've already checked the perimeter of Triple L and Diablo's?" Hank asked the group.

"Yeah, I had Diesel and Wildcard ride the perimeter for the Triple L with one of the ranch hands. Cortez, Raso and I went and talked to Blakely Jr and drove the perimeter of Diablo's with him. There were a few places that looked like someone tampered with the fences, but they weren't down. Wildcard checked the footage from the security cameras at my ranch. He could see someone messing with an area of the back-fence area. When they realized there was a camera around some of the fence area, they hightailed it out of there, but couldn't see any faces. Frank is checking his security footage and will get back to us." Lone informed his boss.

"Have you talked to Culpepper about his perimeter?" Hank asked Lone.

"No. We thought it best that you did, considering how he is." Lone admitted.

"What's the story with this Culpepper guy?" Sgt. Brocard asked Hank.

"The ranch used to belong to the Jameson family. Old man Jameson died of a heart attack a couple of years back. The widow couldn't get the son to come home and take care of the place. Kid was a loose cannon, was always in trouble with the law. Culpepper's father swooped in and bought the place up." Swede informed Alpha Squad.

"Rumor is that the old man and his son are dirty. Supposedly have their hands in the underground criminal world. Word about town is that old man Jameson's son owed Culpepper money, in order to pay off his debt, he talked his mother into giving them the Jameson ranch for cheap." Lone stated, backing up Swede's statement.

"Culpepper's father is an executive big wiz of some kind. Tried to buy up some of the other ranches, got told to take a hike. He came here a while back, before they bought the Jameson place. The older Culpepper got upset when I laughed him out the front door." Hank sighed, sitting down behind his desk. "They aren't the most sociable or the most liked in town."

"Culpepper fired pretty much everyone who worked the ranch when they bought it. They kept on the foreman and two other people but that was it. They let everyone else go when they brought in people from elsewhere to run the ranch. They cause a lot of ruckus in town on the weekends, when they aren't in town, they go into Bozeman. The foreman is a good friend of ours, he's had to drive out there several times to bail them boys out of jail." Swede said, shaking his head. "They have a high turnover rate, that's for damn sure. Every couple of months there's a new crew coming in. I think in the two years since they've had that place, only a handful are still there from the original crew that the fool bought in."

"Culpepper Sr has never been seen in town or on the ranch other than when he initially bought it. No one goes out there though. The Sheriff doesn't even go onto the land, they supposedly have their own security, hired mercs." Hank states, looking at the women.

"Oh, really now?" Sgt Brocard states, with a smirk.

"Hmm, how about I bring out my alter ego Sarge? I mean I know how that world works. I can deal with it for one day." Pratt offers.

"Are you sure about that Red? I know you hate that world after the shit you went through with your family." Sgt Brocard says, looking at Pratt, making sure she *was* okay.

"This is for Emma. If it was anyone else, I'd say fuck it and let Hank have fun. For Emma? I'd go into the fires of hell and beat Satan's ass myself to find that kid." Pratt said fiercely.

Hank coughed a laugh as he stood up. "Red, don't do this if you're uncomfortable. I know you think the world of our daughter, but I can't have your husband kicking my ass because you're doing this."

"Hank, Joe can kiss my ass right now. He won't kick your ass, he knows how I am. You're going to be there with me anyways, I've got this." Pratt said, looking Hank confidently in the eyes.

"Alright, then let's do this. How are we going to do this?" Hank said, looking around the room.

CHAPTER 9

THE NEXT DAY, Hank, Pratt, Raso, Sgt. Brocard and Swede drove out to the Twilight Ranch. Informing the guards at the gate that they were there to see Culpepper with Sgt. Brocard, Raso and Pratt identifying themselves as law enforcement, they were shown to Culpepper's office.

"Hank, to what do I owe the pleasure of your company, with the police no less." Jasper Culpepper said, waiving for the group to sit down.

"Culpepper, this is Detectives Pratt and Raso and Sgt. Brocard from the Riverton County Sheriff's Department in San Diego. They are here in Eagle Pass to assist me with the search for my daughter who was kidnapped yesterday." Hank said, introducing the three members of Alpha Squad.

"I heard your daughter was missing. I'm sorry to hear that, I'm sure you understand my confusion as why you and these females are on my doorstep to see me." Culpepper said, waiving his right hand up and down at the detectives.

"Our reason for being here with Mr. Patterson has to do with the course of our investigation." Pratt said, stepping up to Culpepper's desk and leaning on it, palms down. "During the search from where the kidnapper's vehicle was, then went, we found that they may have come onto your land. We followed tracks that led us to some down fences. We're here as a courtesy to ask for your cooperation in this investigation to make sure these men aren't hiding here."

Culpepper looked at Pratt for a few moments then burst into laughter. "You honestly think that these kidnappers or whomever they are actually managed to get onto my land without me knowing about it? The fence was known about, sweet cheeks. So please do me the pleasure of not insulting me in my own home."

"No one is trying to jerk you around

Jasper. As the detective stated, they wanted to make sure it was known. That's all." Hank told Culpepper, trying to calm the situation down.

"Well, I'm sorry to disappoint you, but the fence was known about and is being dealt with. The tire tracks you apparently followed was that from one of our ATVs that a ranch hand took out on a drunken ride last night. He crashed through the fence to get back onto the land. Now, is there anything else you'd like to waste my time with? Hank, I'm sorry your daughter is missing but I have nothing to do with it, nor do I care." Culpepper said, as he stood up then walked to the door to show them out.

The group left Culpepper's office, once they were away from his property. "The bastard is lying." Pratt said, no holds barred.

"You felt that too?" Raso asked her partner.

"Damn skippy. He has an issue with women in authority, that much is apparent. But I agree with Pratt, Culpepper is lying. Those tracks were not from an ATV. Cortez took photos of those tracks and unless those machines can get kit lifts on them, no one in their right mind would waste the money to make an ATV useless like that." Sgt. Brocard said, shaking her head.

"Sarge is right. Messing with the ATV's makeup will make the vehicle unstable." Raso confirmed.

"They are right, Hank. Culpepper was lying his ass off in there. He knows who it was that messed up his fence and knows it wasn't an ATV. That jackass knows more than he's telling us." Swede fumed.

"Brocard, can you have Cortez and Logan meet us at the site where my daughter was kidnapped. I want to see exactly what they saw." Hank said, looking over at Swede.

Cortez, York, Lone and Wildcard met up with Hank and the others. They stood around discussing the tracks, going over the photos and what each person thinks, Cortez and Wildcard led Swede and Hank to the tracks so they could follow them the same as they done before, straight up to Culpepper's ranch.

"They knew the lay of this land." Swede concluded.

"That's what we are thinking too. There is no spots that show they slowed down or stopped for any period of time that we could find on the ground. Everything is continuous." Cortez confirmed.

"Still think Culpepper is hiding behind the ass burn about the fence deal?" Swede asked his brother-in-law.

"What would Culpepper gain by kidnapping Emma?" Hank asked Swede.

"Talk you into giving up your land for the life of your daughter?" Lone suggested. "Him and his daddy have been trying to buy up more land to add to theirs. They've made several offers for Triple L and Diablo's land, but we've both turned him down." Lone answered.

"Doesn't make sense though. I agree with Hank. No attacks or attempted kidnappings have happened to the Triple L or Diablo's. Had there that happened to either ranch, then I could believe Emma's kidnapping being related to Culpepper going after the land. But Hank's ranch is thirty minutes away. Hank's place doesn't even connect to yours, Diablo's Ranch or the Twilight in anyway. Wouldn't make sense for him to buy out Hank's." Pratt stated, shaking her head.

"I agree with Red, it doesn't make sense to try and go after my land like that. If Culpepper and his father did their homework, they know about the Brotherhood Protection and know I'd never sell, I'd just go after him, money or not." Hank confirmed.

"If these people are as good as they claim they are, they would have done their home-work on Hank. Anyone who really knows Hank would know that kidnapping Emma wouldn't work, Hank would have his people hunt them down then take them out. I think Culpepper knows more than he's admitting." Raso said, wiping her brow and looking around the land.

Hank looked towards the fence and looked for the security cameras that Culpepper said would be out here, just as his phone rang. "Patterson"

"Hank, it's Bird."

"What's up Birdman?"

"Rainman is gone. Cops say it's an overdose."

"What the fuck? Rainman has never used drugs in his life! He hated that shit because of what his brother put the family through. It's the reason he became a SEAL." Hank said heatedly.

"I know that man. I'm just relaying what the cops are saying. I managed to get into his apartment, the fucking place is trashed." Big Bird informed Hank.

"Wasn't he still active?" Hank asked, confused.

"He just came back Stateside two days ago. He made mention of putting in his retirement papers instead of reenlisting when the time came."

"I talked to him about that when I spoke with him a couple of months ago. Made him an offer to come join me out here in Montana." Hank said on a heavy sigh. "Thanks man keep me updated on his funeral arrangements. Let me know what else you find out from the cops."

"Will do. Thought I'd let you know."

Hank hung up the phone as he lowered his head to his chest. "Damn it, just what I need."

"Did I hear you correctly, Rainman is gone?" Swede asked confused.

"Yeah, Bird says it was a drug overdose." Hank confirmed, angry.

"Bullshit. Rainman would never touch shit. Hell, the son-of-a-bitch wouldn't even take fucking pain meds when he got shot in Afghanistan on that op that went to hell." Swede said, just as heated.

"I'm sorry Hank. Where was he stationed?" Pratt asked, rubbing Hanks arm, offering comfort.

"He was out of Little Creek." Swede answered, pacing, clearly agitated.

Hank let out a heavy sigh. "Just hitting hard right now. I just got back the other day from burying Jug, missed hearing about Shepard, now I'm having to bury Rainman."

"Wait, you've had to bury three SEAL team members recently?" York questioned, looking at her teammates.

"Yeah, Shepard supposedly was gunned down during a gas station robbery gone bad in San Diego about three weeks ago. He was grabbing some snacks and a couple of beers to take home after just coming back from being down range." Hank informed the women, rubbing the back of his neck.

"Jughead was killed when his car went off the side of a cliff heading home to see his mom after being forced to take some RnR because he was taking Sheps death pretty hard. We were in Colorado for the funeral when Emma was kidnapped." Swede continued with the information sharing.

"Hank, did you serve with these guys? I know I'm just a SEAL wife, I'm still learning the dynamics of how you guys operate." Pratt asked, looking at the two men then her teammates.

"Not on a full-time basis. Now and then, they would need specialized teams to go and handle specific cases. It's not uncommon for specials teams to be put together depending on the situation. Kind of like some of the OPS that were done in the middle east." Hank answered, confused. "Why?"

"What are you thinking there Red? Them wheels are starting to smoke with all that running you're making that hamster do." Sgt. Brocard said.

"Doesn't it sound strange that three Navy SEAL teammates are now dead, three of them still active, all three considering leaving and yet they wind up killed shortly after coming home from an op?" Pratt said, working her thoughts out loud.

"Shit, she's right. We were already thinking that with the information that was coming in about Jugheads car." Swede said, looking at Hank.

"But why would someone be trying to take us out? There are no foreigners here in Eagle Pass and we've never killed any Americans during our assignments. We would have been benched for friendly fire until their investigation was completed. We've never been under any investigations." Hank said, getting frustrated.

"Hank, when was the last time you saw these guys?" Pratt asked, looking over at Hank.

"We did our last mission about six months before the mission that ended my career as a SEAL." Hank said, thinking back. "So, it's been probably four or five years since I last saw them. We've talked on the phone now and then in that time. I spoke with Shepard two months ago, day before he went down range. I offered him a job with us since he's been talking about leaving the Teams. He was due to fly out here in a couple of months and stay for a few weeks. Said he wanted to check it out before he decided one way or the other what he was going to do."

"Ok, not to speak ill of the crap situation that Hank has been dealt, but what does this guy's death have to do with Emma missing?" Wildcard asked the group.

"Nothing, sorry we're getting off track." Sgt. Brocard stated, smiling at Wildcard. "Sorry Hank."

"Actually, it may be connected. Hank,

were the other three guys married, have children or girlfriends they were serious about?" Rameriez asked.

"No. They had the same mentality a lot of SEALs have when they are active." Hank answered.

"What's that? Fuck everything coming or going while they are active?" Raso questioned with a laugh.

"SEALs have a high divorce rate. Many women can't handle the constant deployments or the unknown. SEALs can't talk about where they are going or where they've been. They can't confirm or deny anything we may hear about on the news. A lot of women feel like they are alone or accuse the SEAL of cheating on them, using the missions as an excuse." Pratt said, looking over at the men with a smile.

"One thing I've learned with Highlander, when he comes home, I let him lead. I follow his movements to know how to proceed. If the mission was successful and not any issues, then he usually is happy, he's glad to be home. The guys tend to have a beer after landing. If there was an issue, he can be distant because he has a lot on his mind. Many women can't deal with that so many of the SEALs aren't in relationships, unless it's a friend's with bene-fits or a one-night stand deal." Pratt informed her teammates.

"Your point?" Wildcard asked, shuffling from foot to foot.

"*IF* and it's a big if, this is the work of the same person or people, it makes sense. These three SEALs didn't have a family. As much as I hate to say this, it makes sense why he killed them. Hank has a wife and a child. If he wants to make Hank suffer, the best way to do that to a man who has the world, is disrupt that world." Pratt said, explaining for Wildcard.

"Son-of-a-bitch. Disrupt his world, take his child and threaten to kill the wife. Show a Spec Ops operator that a regular civilian can outsmart him." York said, baffled.

"Exactly. Law enforcement, military and Special Forces all have specialized training. SEALs and Delta Force more than others. The biggest way to insult them is to outsmart their training and take their family." Raso agreed, catching on to what Pratt was concluding.

"So, we're thinking that this is someone who has an issue with Hank and his SEAL team?" Wildcard asked, shocked at their train of thought.

"I'll admit it's far-fetched, but it's making sense now. These three guys were still active duty, just returning from being down-range and now they are dead. Hank is retired, has a life that he's made outside of the SEALs, so they can mess with him longer. The others had none, plus one never knows when they would go down-range again." Pratt stated, looking at the group. "Look, I don't know about Lone or Wildcard, but since they working for you Hank, I can assume they were Spec Ops. I know how you guys get called at a moment's notice. This guy probably felt he couldn't play with them like he can you. We need to find a way to look at past missions and see what could cause someone to come to the US and fuck with you like this."

"Alright, let me make some calls, see what I can get released. These guys weren't my normal team. Swede was on my assigned SEAL Team. Shepard, Rainman and Jughead were from other SEAL teams, from both the east and the west coast. We only worked together on a few special assignments when needed." Hank said, running his fingers through his hair, sighing heavy.

"That would be hundreds of missions, we

don't have that kind of time for Emma." Lone said, seething. "Let alone, you ladies don't have the clearance for that kind of information. So, what is your agenda?"

"First off, asshat, Hank already said they weren't his 'normal team.'" Diesel said, sneering at Lone, using air quotes. "We'd *only* need to look at the missions where they all worked together. Well, Hank and Swede would."

"Enough you two. Stow the pissing match. Hank, let's see if you can get permission to discuss *those* cases. It's connected to that team. If we can find a connection, then we can figure out how to beat this bastard." Pratt said, walking up to Hank and looking him in the eyes.

"Shit Hank, we've done maybe a dozen missions with that team." Swede said, hands on his hips, glancing around, agitated.

"I'll make some calls." Hank said, walking away.

"Ok, let's give Hank time to make those calls. It's getting late, let's meet back up at Hank's place tomorrow morning. Everyone, get some rest." Sgt. Brocard told her team.

CHAPTER 10

"I'M GOING to call Highlander. If these three guys were active duty SEALs, then he may have known them. I'll see what I can find out about them. I only told him we were leaving out of San Diego for a case, didn't tell him that we were leaving the state." Pratt told her team, sheepishly.

"Someone's gonna get a spanking!" Diesel sang from the back seat.

"And the problem with that is?" Pratt asked her teammate with a smirk on her face.

"Shoot me now!" Raso grumbled, banging her head against the SUV window as Pratt pulled out her phone to dial her husband's number.

"Hello lass, how's work?" Lt. Joe 'Highlander' MacLeod asked his wife.

"Well, our case is in Eagle Pass, Montana." Pratt said, cringing.

"Ah, so ye are in Montana?" Highlander asked, lowering his tone a little.

"Yeah. Umm, so have you've probably heard about the two SEALs that died recently?" Pratt asked, concern in her voice.

"Chicken shit" Diesel mocked whispered, causing Raso to laugh out.

"Aye, I have. What does that have to do with ye being in Montana?"

"Umm well, we think that they are all connected and that the same person who murdered them also kidnapped Hank Patterson's daughter Emma. By the way, he asked for Alpha Squad's help and we couldn't say no!" Pratt said, rushing to get everything out, flipping her teammates off at their laughter in the background.

"Wait a minute, did ye say that Hank's daughter was kidnapped?" Highlander asked quickly, his voice going up in concern.

"Um, yea. He was away for one of the funerals in Colorado when Sadie was attacked. We are out of our depths here, but we plan on helping Hank and his men any way we can." Pratt affirmed to her husband quietly.

"Aye, I know ye lasses will love." Highlander said affectionately.

"I'm worried about Hank though. He got a call today about someone named Rainman supposedly overdosing. He nor Swede are buying it."

"Lass, did ye just say Rainman overdosed?" Highlander asked with shock in his voice.

"Uh huh. Hank got the call while we were out. He's not handling this well. We think it all may be connected." Pratt went on to explain the theory she and the team came up with to her husband.

"Lass, Mac, Snake and I will be there in the morning. We knew the other two men as well. We will help any way we can." Highlander told his wife firmly.

"What about…" Pratt started to ask.

"My parents surprised us, well me, today when they called from the airport to say they were in the States visiting their American children. They will watch all three wee barrens with glee."

"Tell your parents thank you and I'm sorry that I'm not there to see them right now. I'll see you in the morning handsome." Pratt said as she hung up the phone.

"Great, we're being invaded." Raso groaned as she slid down in her seat.

Early the next morning, Highlander, Matthew 'Mac' Johnson, Blakely 'Snake' Evans, and Tony 'Doc' McDonald knocking on Pratt's hotel room door.

"Someone really wants to fucking get stabbed, violently, first thing this morning!" Raso growled as she answered the door.

"Promises, promises sexy lady!" Snake said with a little too much cheer in his voice.

"Babe, if you value your teammate's lives, zip his ass up or you and the kids will be visiting me in jail, cause I'm going to kill his ass." Pratt growled from her bed.

"Damn boss man, you didn't warn us that the hot bride was a grouch first thing in the morning." Snake said laughing, after whistling at the two women.

Chuckling, Highlander caught his wife as she jumped out of bed to go after Snake while Mac grabbed Raso to keep her from maiming Snake as well. "Snake, if you value your balls, I'd shut it if I were you" Doc said, warning his buddy, laughing.

"What time did ye get to bed last night

lass?" Highlander asked his wife, after giving her a quick kiss hello.

"I think we finally called it a night about one am. Diesel managed to pull up some aerial maps of the area here where Sadie was attacked. Sgt Brocard, Raso and I made some calls to San Diego PD and to Virginia Beach PD to see if we can get copies of the police reports for the three deaths to go over so we could see what we can find." Pratt explained to the men.

"Any luck?" Mac asked, moving to sit in the chair inside the room.

"More questions than answers. Maybe it's just me, but I don't see how this person got the drop on three SEALs. I mean you guys are on alert 24/7, even on domestic soil. This asshat managed to get to three SEALs. It just doesn't make sense to me." Raso said, admitting her hesitance with the information provided.

"Ok, let's hear it." Doc said, sitting on Raso's bed, leaning forward to listen.

Raso and Pratt told the four SEALs their theory and why they questioned the information that both departments provided on the attack of the SEALs. All four men, despite knowing the women, were impressed with their theory and train of thoughts. They listened, asked a few questions here and there, then listened some more. When all was said and done, the four men had to agree in the end that the three deaths didn't make sense, despite the facts about the case.

"Ye both have great points and are right. It's hard to get over on a SEAL, hell any Special Forces operator for that matter, especially after we just returned from being down range. I agree something had to have happened for these men to let their guard down. What are the chances of ye getting the footage of the robbery?" Highlander asked his wife.

"Slim to none. According to the detective handling the case in Virginia Beach, the camera where Shepard was shot wasn't working, yet where the cashier was located, it was working. Unfortunately, nothing is visible towards Shepard's location from that camera." Pratt answered, shaking her head.

"These guys knew to keep their faces out of the range of the camera." Raso confirmed.

"What about the other two?" Snake asked.

"Still waiting to hear back from Colorado law enforcement. I made a call to someone I know there to see if they can't check a few things out for us. SDPD is taking their sweet time getting back to us, so I reached out to Dom to see if he could find out anything." Pratt said, getting up from the bed.

"Where are ye going lass?" Highlander asked, voice getting husky.

"Well since you woke us up, I'm going to go grab a shower so I can get dressed and get some grub. You ok with that?" Pratt asked her husband in a snarky tone.

"Umm I'm going to go wake up Diesel and see if I can borrow their shower since you're gonna use that one right now." Raso said, quickly getting up to grab a few things before heading to the door.

"Yeahhhh, ummm Doc, Snake, lets go grab some coffee and grub for these ladies." Mac said, pulling on Snake who was engrossed in the stare down between Highlander and Pratt.

"Lass, I understand ye are cranky first thing in the morning, but do I need to remind ye what happens when ye get sassy with me?" Highlander asked, tone low and controlled.

"Not like you'll do anything anyway." Pratt snarked as she stared Highlander down. When he made a move to leave, Pratt sighed. "No. I'm sorry, just frustrated with this case and didn't get much sleep before you guys showed up." Pratt admitted, sheepishly.

"Come here lass." Highlander said huskily.

"No, don't wanna." Pratt said pouting.

"Lass, if I get back up, I'll have to spank that arse." Highlander said, grinning.

"Promise?" Pratt asked, perking up.

"No, because if I spank ye arse, it won't go any further." Highlander said, sternly.

Pratt puttered over to where her husband was sitting on the bed. "Ok, I'm here."

Highlander reached up and palmed his wife's face, looking into her eyes. "What else is bothering ye lass?"

"Nothing. I've missed you and I'm worried sick about Emma." Pratt said, leaning down, placing her lips onto her husbands for a small kiss.

"Aye, lass, I've missed ye too. I hated having to be away from ye these last several months."

"I knew what I signed up for when I said yes to being with you, Joe. You're a SEAL first and foremost. Will be until the day you die."

"Ah lass, I don't deserve ye sometimes." Highlander murmured as he took his wife's lips.

Palming Pratt's face, Highlander brought

his wife's lips back to his, kissing her gently at first with small pecks. Highlander swallowed her gasp when he ran his tongue over her lips. Their kiss became heated as Pratt leaned into her husband, running her fingers into his longer than Navy regulated hair, tightening her grip.

Highlander leaned back onto the bed, pulling Pratt down with him, as he continued to drink from her lips. He moved his hand from her cheek to her nape, holding her head in place as his free hand went to her hips to help her straddle him.

Pratt followed her husband down onto the bed, straddling him, feeling his steel hardness against her. Slightly rubbing herself against him, Pratt mewled at the feeling it caused to race through her body. Untangling herself from Highlander, Pratt sat up, looking into his eyes as she pulled her sleep shirt off.

Highlander's eyes grew dark with desire as he realized what Pratt was wearing. It always made him catch his breath when he saw his wife wearing one of his shirts to sleep in. He had asked her once if she needed new night clothes, she nonchalantly told him no and that she had plenty.

Without realizing she was giving away her

best friend during a conversation, Raso made the statement that Pratt became mushy when he was away on deployments because she wouldn't sleep without one of his shirts and a pair of his boxers to feel like he was next to her.

Highlander leaned up and latched his mouth onto one of Pratt's nipples, licking, teasing and sucking hard, bringing it to a hard peak. Loving the sound of his wife's moans, he moved to the other breast and started his teasing of that one. Highlander knew that teasing his wife's breasts drove her wild. Ever since the twin's birth, her nipples have been more sensitive than ever.

Highlander fought hard to maintain his control with Pratt's gyration on his hard cock. Taking a hard peak between his thumb and forefinger, he tweaked her nipple as he looked into her eyes, watching them cloud over from desire, darker than his. Highlander leaned down taking her breast back into his mouth, teasing her more. Loving the feeling of his wife gripping his hair, scratching at his neck and upper back, getting lost in her desire.

Pratt gripped Highlander's hair hard, pulling him off her breast to pull his shirt over his head. She sealed her lips to his. Kissing him like a woman dying of thirst. Pratt fed on Highlander's lips as she pushed him down onto the bed, then stood up. Pratt then gripped unbuttoned his jeans, then pulled them off, along with his boxers, shoes and socks. Looking at her husband with a smirk, she leaned over him, placing a kiss on his washboard abs, licking and nibbling her way down.

Highlander fought the urge to surge upward and pull her off of him when he felt Pratt's mouth cover the head of his cock. Gripping the covers on the bed, he groaned when he felt her tongue tease the head of his cock. Highlander arched his neck and bit back a loud curse when Pratt took him as far into her mouth as he could go, swallowing a few times in the process as she sucked and licked his hardness.

"Son of a bitch, lass" Highlander groaned.

When Pratt swallowed with his cock hitting the back of her throat, Highlander groaned. "Fuck babe" Pulling himself up into a sitting position, he used one hand to grab Pratt's hair and the other her upper arm, pulling her off his cock before he embarrassed himself. He wasn't going to waste six months of waiting to be with his wife down her throat. He twisted as he pulled her off, tossing her onto the bed.

Pratt screamed out when Highlander teased her clit with this tongue before he went lower and started using his tongue in her core, like he plans to use his cock. Forcing himself to slow down, slowly driving his wife mad, teasing, licking and nibbling on her outer lips. He alternated between licking around her clit and around her core, never really touching either again just yet.

When Pratt started begging Highlander to stop teasing her, he finally used his fingers to drive her over the edge as he sucked her clit at the same time. Before she had a chance to come down from her powerful orgasm, Highlander drew himself up over her, pulling her right leg with him as he thrust hard and deep inside. Holding still to give Pratt a moment to adjust to his size, he leaned down and kissed her passionately.

"Fuck lass, ye feel so damn good. It's been too damn long since I've felt your heat." Highlander said huskily.

"Too damn long. I miss feeling you inside me." Pratt murmured against his lips as she wiggled her hips, trying to get him to move.

Highlander used his free hand to swat her hip. "Stay still Laura, or this will be over before either of us get started. I've been without ye taste and ye heat for six fucking months, don't rush this."

Highlander slowly started moving, pulling all the way out, looking into Pratt's eyes before he thrust back inside. Slow and hard, staring into each other's eyes had them both panting and moaning before long. The intensity nearly drove them both insane before long.

Pratt reached up with a hand and palmed Highlander's face, bringing his lips back down to hers so she could kiss him hungrily. Pratt started to deepen the kiss the closer to her orgasm she got. Feeling her inner walls starting to spasm, Highlander started to thrust in and out faster, as he felt his own orgasm starting to tingle at the base of his spine, working its way up.

Pratt grabbed Highlander by the nape with one hand and then gripped the skin of his back with her other, scratching his back and neck as her orgasm exploded more powerful than the first one, she broke the kiss and bit down onto his shoulder, screaming into his skin. Feeling her teeth sink into his skin, Highlander lost control, pounding into his wife's heat, screaming out her name as he emptied himself deep inside of her.

They held onto each other, trying to catch their breaths for several minutes. After twenty minutes of relaxing, Highlander looked over at his wife and smiled. "Ye okay lass? I didn't hurt ye did I?"

"Never. I'm sorry I bit you. We need to get it cleaned so it doesn't get infected." Pratt said, shyly.

Highlander tipped her chin to force her to look into his eyes. "Lass, never feel ashamed for biting me, scratching me or anything when we are in the middle of our passions. I love feeling your nails sinking into me, ye biting me or even hearing ye scream my name. It makes me lose my control. I'm barely fighting that same control when I'm inside of ye. So never feel ashamed for whatever you feel the need to do."

"Same goes for you mister. I know you held back just now." Pratt said, leaning up and kissing him ever so briefly.

"Aye, ye caught me lass. But since we are in a hotel, ye teammates and mine on the other side of the wall, I didn't feel like sharing your sounds with anyone until we get home.

Then I can truly take my time with ye." Highlander said, winking at his wife as he swatted her behind. "Now my beautiful siren, it's time to get ye arse up and let's get a shower before the busybodies return with breakfast."

"They should be back already, unless they've eaten it all." Pratt grumbled.

"All the more reason to get up and get showered so we can get some grub too"

CHAPTER 11

HIGHLANDER AND PRATT got a quick shower, cleaning each other up with a couple more orgasms before they met up with everyone for a quick bite to eat. Taking three SUVs, everyone headed to the Patterson Ranch. After the initial shock, back slapping and a few pleasantries were exchanged, everyone headed into Hank's office.

"What the hell Highlander? When did you degenerates get into town?" Hank asked, still getting over his surprise of seeing his fellow SEALs.

"This morning. My lass called last night to inform me that she wouldn't be home for a few more days and what was going on. I'd only gotten to kiss her goodbye when she left for work after being gone for six months," Highlander said as he gave his wife the stink eye.

"Shit, I'm sorry, I called them for help. I'm going insane worrying about Emma…"

"Hank, don't ye dare apologize for asking for my wife or her team's help. I understand what is going on. Since I've met my lass and Cody, and now I'm a father of two of my own, I get it. If it had been Cody, Willie or little Rileyh, I'd be where ye are." Highlander admitted, slinging his arm over his wife's shoulder, pulling her in as he shuddered at the thought of either one of his children being taken from them.

"Where are the kids now?" Swede asked, looking around the room.

"My parents surprised me with a visit. Their plan was to surprise Red since I was deployed at the time, only I got the surprise since my lass wasn't home. They have the three hellions now." Highlander chuckled. "I swear I don't know who's going to be more overprotective of Rileyh, me, Willie or Cody."

"Lord help that poor girl. It's bad enough she's got this group for aunts when she starts showing an interest in boys, but Lord help that child when you, your SEALs, her uncle Dom or her brothers find out about the boys." Pratt laughed, shaking her head.

"You're damn right about that. Don't forget about her uncles here in Montana. No boy is going be good enough for our girls." Hank laughed a little, then quieted down.

"We will find her Hank. Don't give up on us. Make the call to the Pentagon. While you talk to them, we're going to go and check on Sadie really quick." Pratt said, walking over and giving Hank a big hug before walking out of the office to give them men privacy.

An hour later the group all met back in Hanks office to find out how to proceed forward with their investigation. The mood was somber and quiet. When Hank hung up the phone, Swede walked over and sat on the edge of the desk.

"Well?"

"Just as we expected, Pentagon says no and there's nothing the Admiral will do about it. Says we have to figure this out on our own and from what his sources say, all the key players are gone so there shouldn't be any blow back from any of the missions we handled." Hank said, groaning as he leaned back in his chair.

"There's gotta be a way to find out this information. Don't you guys keep notes or remember any of the missions you've done personally?" Diesel asked Hank and Swede.

"No, most of the time after we debrief it's memories. We either remember or work our asses off to forget." Swede answered, looking over at Hank and the other four SEALs for confirmation.

"Plus, we don't want to chance civilians getting a hold of the information if they were to be snooping around a person's private abode." Snake said, wiggling his eyebrows at the women.

"Keep dreaming jackass!" Raso said, rolling her eyes.

"Abode? Who says that shit?" Diesel asked out loud, shaking her head.

"It's not only that, but we've been out for several years. The last mission we did with these guys was four or five years ago. Why would they wait all this time to come after us?" Hank asked, confused.

"Good question. We need to get ahold of those files. Is there anyone we can call to get the ball rolling?" Rameriez asked, running her fingers through her hair.

"Welllll, there is someone I can call, but Highlander won't like it if I do." Pratt replied, chewing on her lower lip, looking over at her husband.

"Who is it?" Swede asked, quirking an eyebrow, hearing Highlander's low, deep growl after Pratt's comment.

"Oh hell, just give squidward extra head, dress sexy, and offer up more ass than normal." Raso quipped, making vomit faces in the process.

All eight men coughed to hide their laughs when Pratt flipped Raso the middle finger. "Who is it that you can call? Remember they have to be able to override the classification status on these files." Hank reminded Pratt, interested in the conversion.

"Lass, make the call. I'll keep the comments to a minimum. This is for Emma." Highlander said, giving Pratt a smacking kiss. "A couple of years ago, Raso, Cortez, York and my wife assisted in a situation that never made the major news networks because of diplomatic protection or something like that. Since then, they've helped Alpha Squad out in situations like this." Highlander explained to Hank.

"Holy batshit, he's right!" Diesel exclaimed. "Captain Irby called and used him when Pratt and Cortez were kidnapped and taken to Mexico."

Pratt looked over at Hank, then pulled out her phone, hitting a button, then putting her phone on speaker, for everyone to hear. Pratt cracked her knuckles trying to settle her nerves. Not many people, outside her team, the Captain, and her husband knew of her friendship with the person she was calling.

"Blakely"

"Hey Blakely, it's Matthews busy?" Pratt asked, speaking low.

"Well hey there stranger! No, he's sitting here looking at the birth announcement that he received from you and the other half. They are beautiful, just like their mother. Congrats on both your marriage and their birth."

"Awe, thanks handsome. Is there any chance I can talk to him please?" Pratt asked, hesitantly.

"Sure, is everything ok Red?"

"I'm fine. I need a huge favor that only he can help with, for a friend of mine. It's a matter of life and death. Otherwise I wouldn't be asking." Pratt said, trying reign in her desperation.

"I know, hold on beautiful, let me put you on speaker phone."

Pratt looked over at Hank then at her husband, while waiting for Blakely to set settled. "Hank, what was the team called when you all worked together?"

"Gold Team One" Hank answered hesitantly looking over to Swede who nodded.

"Red, everything okay? Blakely said there is an issue."

"Good Morning, President Matthews. I'm so sorry to bother you first thing in the morning."

"Wait a damn minute, did she just say President Matthews? As in the President of the United States of America, President Matthews?" Lone asked Alpha Squad in shock.

"Yep" Diesel responded, popping her 'p'.

"What's going on sweetheart?" President Matthews voice asked over the phone.

"You may not think that in a few minutes." Pratt laughed. "Sir, I have you on speaker phone. I'm in Eagle Pass, Montana, with Hank Patterson and three members of his team now, as well as Highlander and a few members of his team. Patterson is a former Navy SEAL whose daughter was kidnapped the other day. We strongly believe that it has something to with one of the missions he was on while a part of Gold Team One, more than seven years ago."

"Laura" President Matthews said quietly. "You know I can't give you classified files. I'm sorry. I can do anything else, but that."

"Tony, I'm not asking you to give it to me or to Alpha Squad. I'm asking you to allow Hank to comb through those files since *he* was a part of that team. Help him brainstorm to figure out who is killing other members of that same team and kidnapped his daughter, an eighteen month old child. These monsters took her from her mother's arms, shot at the mother and is torturing Hank with threats of coming back for his wife after they send him his daughter, piece by fucking piece!" Pratt begged, strongly.

"Wait a minute, who is killing who?"

"Someone, whomever is involved in Emma Patterson's abduction, has managed to kill three active duty Navy SEALs shortly after they have returned home from missions. They have managed to make them all look like accidents as well. All three men served with Hank and his brother-in-law, Swede. These two are the only two retired SEALs from that team. The other five were still active duty. Two still remain alive and will stay that way as long as they stay downrange until we catch these fuckers." Pratt answered, anger in her voice.

"Laura, what makes you think it's someone taking this team out?" Blakely asked, confused.

"You really need me to lay it out for you boys?" Pratt asked, frustrated.

"Laura, I know you think I'm being a jerk, but I'm not. If I'm going to wade through classified information, I need to have a plausible reason when I'm getting asked why. Thoughts, unfortunately, aren't good enough reasons to do so."

"You're not a jerk! I just hate the red tape bullshit, sometimes. Therefore, I could never be your wife, Tony. I hate politics and you know better than anyone I have no damn filter." Pratt answered, rolling her eyes at the laughter coming from the phone and her husband's answering growl beside her.

"She's right there, boss man. The Veep demanded you put tape over her mouth that one day and let's not forget the Senator who demanded that she be taught manners, the old-fashioned way." Blakely reminded Pratt with laughter.

"Yeah and that old geezer was told what he could do with his suggestions too. He never did like me, hated it worse when I divorced his dumbass son. I proved I didn't need their money to live on." Pratt said, taking in a deep breath, letting it slowly out of her mouth. "Hank and Swede were both part of Gold Team One. As I said earlier, both men are sitting here in the room with me, so if there are any questions during this conversation, they can help answer them for you.

"Very well, help me understand your train of thought here, Detective Pratt." President Matthews stated, getting serious. Pratt, Hank and the others then proceeded to lay everything out for Blakely and the President about Shepard's death.

"Damn" Blakely's voice sounded through the speaker phone. "But that still doesn't give enough information for the wade through classified files Detective.

"Who said I was done Blakely?" Pratt shot back.

"My question is this, why was it declared a robbery if only this Shepard guy was shot, and nothing but his beer and smokes were taken from the store?"

"Because the store clerk stated that they did ask for money when they first entered the store. Which is when the cashier refused. Even the detective I spoke with said it was confusing, but they were being told to rule it as a robbery that went bad. They are supposed to be getting me a copy of the store feed here in the next day or two. Just wading through the political red tape bullshit. The case is still open but not many leads to go on."

"Alright, you said there were three deaths. Who was next?" President Matthews asked, moving on.

"The second death was Clifford 'Jughead' Winston. Shepard and Jughead were friends, having first met in buds. Despite being put on separate teams, Jughead was put on SEAL Team 5 in San Diego." Pratt went on to give more information on Jughead's case. "I contacted a friend in Colorado last night and asked him to look at Jughead's vehicle. It looked like his brake lines had been tampered with. Not your typical tampering either. Apparently, whoever touched his car changed out the brake hose with a frayed one so that the cops would think he just didn't take care of his car."

"And this SEAL was part of this Gold Team One and was also active duty at the time of his death?"

"Yes sir. He had just returned home from a mission and was ordered to take several days of RnR to get his head back into the game. Both Shepard and Jughead had one year left on their contract before they had to decide to either reenlist or retire. According to Hank, he spoke with Shepard two months ago about coming to Montana and working for him. The offer was also extended to Jughead around the same time."

"The third death?" Blakely asked, quietly.

"The third death was reported last night, a Roger 'Rainman' Hayes. He was with SEAL Team 4, stationed in Norfolk, along with Shepard. His death is being ruled a drug overdose which the Navy, Hank and Swede are saying is bullshit. We all know the shit-storm the SEALs went through with the media when it was stated that there was a heavy drug problem among the SEALs. SEALs are drug tested now at random times, and they don't get told when either. Both Hank and Swede said Rainman was venomously against drugs. The man wouldn't even take a Tylenol for Christ sake. Now he's dead with a drug overdose. I agree with them, it's bullshit. I honestly think someone is trying to take out Gold Team One. There's still two more members who are active duty. Hank made a call this morning and it's being handled to keep them overseas until we can get this dealt with."

"Okay, I can give you that. But Laura, if that was the case, why haven't they tried to take out this Swede and Hank person?" President Matthews asked, hitting the question everyone had.

"My honest opinion? Because Hank and Swede are no longer active duty, they have time to mind fuck them and drive them insane. The others, they were still active duty, and no one knew when they would have to go downrange again. They haven't been able to get to Swede because they put his wife and ranch on lockdown. He works with Hank and is part co-owner of the Brotherhood Protectors Agency. They have damn good security. They struck Hank while he was out of state at Jughead's funeral. His wife was driving their daughter back home after a day out in Bozeman with their daughter. They didn't take her from home since they had to have known about Hank's security. At the time, no one put two and two together to realize what it was until Rainman's death."

"Holy shit! She just hit the hail on the head. Had they got to them here, we'd have been able to catch them. Where they attacked Sadie, she was alone on a road that's not often used unless you're going to one of the ranches or into town." Swede realized Pratt's train of thought.

"Shit sir, she's got a point. Someone is taking out these guys and they have a baby. She's laid it out and despite the way it looks, we both know these women look at things we may not. I tend to agree with her." Blakely told his boss, discussing it openly for everyone to hear through the phone.

"Yeah, that's why I keep trying to get her to dump the squid and come marry me so she can help me deal with these assholes on Capitol Hill."

"That squid is right here sir. I will gladly forget who ye are and kick ye arse."

"Yeah, no thanks. Can you please help?" Pratt pleaded.

"Mr. Patterson?" The President said after a brief chuckle.

"Yes, Mr. President."

"Please, call me Tony. Sounds like we're going to become acquainted. Laura said your brother-in-law was also on the team with you?"

"Yes, sir. Axel 'Swede' Svenson was with me on the teams, both my home team as well as Gold Team sir."

"Alright, get my number from Laura, and then give me several hours. I'm going to make some calls and see what I can do. Both of you need to be ready to go through these files so we can find out who the hell is targeting you so we can get your little girl back. Laura, I know you and your team are going to do everything else you can to make that happen. For the love of all that is holy, please be safe. My daughter would kill me if anything happened to you and your team. The nightly calls from you ladies are the highlight of her life."

"Yes sir, thank you sir." Alpha Squad said in union, cheering and high fiving each other.

"Holy shit, you guys are friends with the President himself?" Wildcard chuckled, shaking his head.

"Yep, he's a huge supporter of the task force. Especially after they saved his daughter, and despite who she is, they still treat the kid as one of their own." Doc smiled at this team leader's wife.

"Well, let's get busy while we wait for the big man to get those wheels turning." Sgt. Brocard said loudly.

CHAPTER 12

"HEY HOSS, the third body is down. They discovered his body sooner than we planned but they believe the drug overdose." Bad guy two informed his partner.

"Do you have the cover story paid as well? She has to be believable or this isn't going to work."

"Yeah, the hooker showed up at the apartment claiming the guy arranged for them to meet up. She showed them the text about a party, just the two of them. I made sure it was all sent from his phone before I gave him the final dosage."

"Good, it's all coming to head. I can't get to Svenson since he's staying at Patterson's place. He's got his wife sequestered there too.

We'll plan our time with the last two people and then we'll finish off Svenson and Patterson as a twofer."

"Have you heard any more on their investigation into the brat's disappearance?"

"I know there's discord in the ranks. The men Patterson has working for him don't like the fact he brought in the broads from San Diego. Thinks it makes them look like they can't handle shit."

"What does the boss man think of the whole thing?" Bad guy two asked laughing.

"He was hot to trot when Patterson showed up with those bitches and asked him for the video of his property to see if we came onto the land. Told them to take a flying leap. Took all he had not to punch the fat chick."

"Bitches! They think they can handle a man's world but start crying when a man puts them in their places."

"They won't be doing that whining shit for long. Boss man is biding his time before he gives the order to take them out. He's giving us time to get the rest of the shit dealt with before he does. He wants it to look like an accident"

"I can't wait until this is over with so we can get the fuck out of this sorry ass town. I want back in the real city where the women are better lays than these desperate chicks."

"This is going to be fun" Bad guy one laughed, clapping bad guy two on the back as he walked out the door.

DAY five of Emma's disappearance found Alpha Squad, Hank, Swede, the SEALs, Wildcard and Lone were in Hank's office going over what Hank and Swede remembered off the top of their heads. Swede, Hank, Highlander, Doc, Mac and Snake talked to each other in code if something didn't pan out in their thoughts before they spoke up for everyone else. While they were talking about possibilities, Pratt's phone rang.

"Detective Pratt"

"Laura, it's Tony. Where are you?"

"Good morning Sir, I'm at Hank's house. We're going over what he and Swede remember of their past missions with Gold Team. Why? Were you able to get access?"

"Can you put me on speakerphone?"

"Um, yeah, sure hold on. Ok, you're on speakerphone now."

"Good morning everyone. Mr. Patterson, I

have some good news and even better news. The good news is I was able to grant access to the files that were related to Gold Team One, for you and Mr. Svenson to go through."

"That's awesome news, so what's better than that?" Pratt asked, confused.

"Blakely is on his way to Montana with the file. He is going to be assisting you with the search for the little girl, along with two of his best agents. I want this bastard found and I want to make sure you guys have every available resource available to take them down."

"Are you shitting me? You're seriously sending Blakely this way to help us find Emma? Oh my God, Tony, thank you so much. I love you!!! I mean not that kind of love. I mean I'm not leaving Joe to marry you or anything, but you know, sister slash friend love and all that." Pratt said, rambling in a panic, looking over at her husband, causing everyone to laugh.

"Always ruining my dreams, Red." President Matthews laughed. "One of these days you'll cave when I ask."

"Well, if given the choice of kissing ass and having to play nice or blowing shit up, no offense sir, but I'd rather blow shit up while pissing people off. My resting bitch face doesn't play nice with some of the idiots you are forced to hobnob with."

"Ain't that the truth! Preach it girl!" Diesel hollered out in the background.

President Matthews laughed heartily. "I can honestly say I miss you ladies. Your honesty and straight to the point attitudes, while one and the same, is refreshing with all the bullshit I deal with here in the White House. Blakely left DC early this morning, around 0600 hours. He should be at your destination within the hour or so. He's on his way with two other highly trusted agents. Don't hurt them too bad ladies. Mr. Patterson, I hope the files you needed help you in the search for your daughter."

"Thank you, Mr. President. I appreciate your help, more than you know." Hank said, smiling over at Pratt.

For the two hours, the group looked through notes and brainstormed. Ideas were thrown around and discarded. Finally, around noon, Blakely and the two extra agents arrived at Hank's house.

"What the hell Blakely, did you get lost?" Pratt asked, laughing as she shook hands with Blakely?

"Got a flat tire on the rental. Had to wait for a tow truck and the new rental for about an hour. Then when we got close to this place, saw a little elderly lady on the side of the road, dealing with a flat, so we stopped to help her out."

"Aw, aren't you just the sweetest thang?" Pratt said, batting her eye lashes at Blakely.

"Bitch" Blakely joked.

"That's Detective Bitch, Agent Asshole." Pratt joked back. "Anywho, Hank, Wildcard, Swede and Lone. You already know the rest of my team, Highlander, Mac, Doc and Snake." Pratt introduced everyone in the room, pointing them out. "Everyone, this is special agent Frank Blakely bodyguard to the main man himself. Sorry I only know special agent Jeremy Collins. You are?"

"Hi ma'am, I'm special agent Joseph Johns."

"Oh shit, current hot stuff hubby's name mixed with the ex-demon hubby's name. Talk about an explosive fuck!" Diesel shivered, causing everyone to laugh.

"I always knew ye thought I was hot." Highlander said, winking at Diesel.

"Ugh, barf dude!" Raso quipped, shaking her head.

"So, how's this going to work?" Lone asked the group.

"Those of us not privileged enough to look through the classified information will continue to do solid old-fashioned investigation. Swede, Hank, Blakely, Collins and Johns will go through the files in the briefcase. Hopefully something will click with the guys and I won't look like an overactive freak with my train of thoughts."

"You weren't the only one who's thoughts went there, Red." Raso commented, backing Pratt up. "As soon as Hank mentioned the third SEAL death, that just isn't normal on home soil, I thought the same thing. There's got to be something in one of those files. How many are there to go through?"

"The Pentagon found eighteen files total, that were related to Gold Team One." Blakely answered, pulling files from the secured briefcase. "We'll start with the very first assignment that you guys did and then work our way up to the last assignment you guys did."

"Works for me. If it's okay with you, Swede was also on Gold Team One, our demo expert, he can help assist with what I may have forgotten."

"Works for me too. Will probably help get through the files faster." Blakely said, nodding at the files.

"Alright, you guys do what needs to be done. Hopefully within the next couple of hours, we'll have an idea of what the hell we are going up against and who the hell has my daughter."

"We will find her Hank. There's no doubt about that." Pratt said, strongly.

"Alright ladies, let's get ready to go, we're going to do some investigations on our end, as if we were still in San Diego." Sgt. Brocard announced to the group of women.

"All ready. So exactly what are we doing? We're pretty much at a dead end here." Rameriez stated.

"Ramz is right. Everything is hanging on Hank finding something in those files." Diesel agreed.

"True, but while Hank and Swede go through the files with Blakely and the other two agents, the rest of us are going to cause a stir and piss off some rich people. I think this Culpepper guy is hiding something and knows more than he's let on. So, it's time to live up to our name as pit bulls and dig in this fucker's ass." Pratt informed the room.

"Are the SEALs going to help us with this part or are they going to hang with Hank and Swede while they go through the files?" York asked Pratt.

"Actually, we're going to split up, myself and Mac will be assisting Hank while Doc and Snake will be assisting ye lasses." Highlander said from his seat across the room by Hank.

"Maybe we should have Brody look into Culpepper since Brody's family is pretty wealthy. He can probably find out some information that we don't have." Raso suggested.

"Good point. While my family is well to do, Brody's family is obnoxiously rich." Pratt agreed.

"Wait, the guy that works the front area of a police precinct is from a filthy rich family? I mean, wow! He doesn't have to work and yet he slums it in a police office?" Blakely asked, in shock.

All eight members of Alpha Squad flipped Blakely off, causing the other men in the room to laugh. "First of all, asshole, I think the same about you!" Pratt said, smirking, "Second, he does it to piss his parents off, since they demand he work for daddy's company and marry a wealthy woman. Kinda reminds me of someone else I know."

"What's wrong with being married to a rich chick?" Agent Johns asked, causing Blakely, Highlander, Mac, Doc, Snake and Alpha Squad to burst into fits of laughter. Hank, Swede, Wildcard, Lone and Agent Collins looked at each other confused, causing them to laugh harder.

"Sorry, that was hilarious. Cute, but hilarious. I'll have to tell Brody that one. Hank, you should ask Highlander about his first meeting with Brody." Pratt said, wiping the tears from her eyes.

"Och, let's not. That is a recurring issue when I want to come visit ye at work, lass." Highlander groaned.

"What does that have to do with Agent Johns question?" Lone asked, looking at the women more confused.

"Lone, you can't be that dumb. Brody refuses to marry a rich woman, key word woman, because he's gay. Very happily gay. His parents have thought for years it was a rebellious phase, like some girls go through, and threaten every year to cut him off. But his grandmother, bless her beautiful soul, is still alive and accepts Brody as he is. She refuses to allow the parents to cut him off." Raso said smiling.

"Brody is wicked smart and damn good with computers. He knows his parents want him at their company to abuse his skills. He also knows the Task Force won't abuse his skills for illegal gains, unless it involves saving one of us or a child." Rameriez added.

"He may just be our human resources, slash admin guy, but make no mistakes, Brody is a huge part of the HTTF. He's our heart and soul." York finished for Alpha Squad.

"Okay, so what about a rich guy to marry?" Agent Collins asked shrugging.

"Oh God, please don't ever ask Brody that question! He says rich men are worse than valley chicks from California." Diesel laughed.

"Not all of them are." Hank answered.

"No, not all of them, but enough. Brody is happy being Brody." Sgt. Brocard responded. "Brody is also the perfect person to dig deeper into Culpepper, while we go talk to him on an official capacity."

"Hell's, we may want to call Captain Irby and give her a heads up about Culpepper. Granted Blakely and the President will back our play, but Culpepper will try to use his money and name with the Sheriff. If we give the Captain a heads up, she'll be prepared for the shit storm. Especially when we inform her that we feel he's involved in Emma's kidnapping." Pratt suggested to Sgt. Brocard.

While Hank and Swede looked through the first two files, Alpha Squad conducted a conference call with Sheriff Phillips, Captain Irby and their Task Force Assistant, Galvin Brody. Laying out their plan and giving the heads up to their upper command, always made their plan of actions easier. It wasn't uncommon for the team to use Brody in their cases, but it was few and far between. Brody gladly accepted the request to assist Alpha Squad without question.

"So, let me get this straight, daddy is a big head honcho who hates women, especially ones with power, has an idiot for a son who is the mole off daddy's tushie." Brody repeated, with his own flair.

"Pretty much." Pratt answered with a chuckle. "We need your ears to see what you can find out about the Culpepper's. We need something we can use against him when we go and confront him."

"Oh, silly ladies, I know exactly who the

Culpepper family is and I have plenty of juicy, factual information that can be used."

For the next hour, Brody informed Alpha Squad of the inside information on the Culpepper family. Hank, Swede, and the Secret Service Agents continued to go through the files, hoping something answered their questions on who has baby Emma.

CHAPTER 13

Hours after the three secret service agents arrived at the Patterson Ranch, a plan was devised on how best to approach Culpepper. Hank and Swede took a small break to go over the aerial photos with the women. Hank dispatched a small group of his men to assist with coverage around Culpepper's Ranch.

The Culpepper Ranch was backed up against a heavily wooded area that covered a large man-made lake in the middle of the tree lines that covered Diablo's Ranch. Members of the Brotherhood Protection were stationed in that area to monitor in case anyone tried to flee. Hank sent Swede with the group to Culpepper's, splitting Alpha Squad into three separate teams.

Lone, Mac, Diesel, Rameriez and Raso were sent to cover the east part of the ranch, making sure no one slipping out towards Lone's ranch. Wildcard, Doc, Snake, York and Cortez were dispatched to the west side of the ranch, which was situated towards another large ranch. Pratt, Highlander, Swede and Sgt. Brocard were the unlucky, or lucky, depending on who you spoke to, participants to go and deal with Culpepper face to face.

"I thought I made myself clear last time…" Culpepper started.

"And now we are here to make ourselves clear." Sgt. Brocard stated, calm, firm and to the point. "These two men are here for your protection. We tried to play nice, and it didn't work, so now, we are here on our terms, and it's not going to be so nice."

"I suggest you watch who you're talking to, bitch." Culpepper sneered.

"It's Sgt. Bitch to you. You see, we did some digging into your father and you, Mr. Culpepper. We found out some very interesting information regarding you both." Pratt said, looking Culpepper in the eyes.

"It's very obvious you whores have no idea who you are dealing with. You're not in San Diego, you're in Eagle Pass, Montana, a totally different world." Culpeper said, in a warning tone in his voice.

"Oh, make no mistake Culpepper, we know exactly who we are dealing with. You see, we know your father runs in a certain crowd back in San Diego. You followed in daddy's footsteps. Yet, you made a very serious mistake when you crossed the line in that same circle, causing daddy to use every favor he had to get you out of trouble. That issue caused daddy to buy land in Eagle Pass. Lo and behold, it was done to keep you out of jail, or even worse, dead. Yet, from what I've heard, either way, jail or not, had you stayed in San Diego, or California for that matter, you'd still have wound up dead." Pratt shrugged, raising an eyebrow, daring Culpepper to deny the allegations.

Culpepper clapped while he let out a belly laugh. "Such a grand tale. You really are amusing sluts and very uneducated it seems."

"Actually Culpepper, it's you it seems is the uneducated one. See, we reached out to the local sheriff, he refused, claiming there were no issues. Nothing new, since we can and have proven that your father was paying him heavily to turn the other cheek where you and your boys were concerned. Oh, and the Sheriff sang like a wee fucking canary on your ass as well." Pratt laughed.

"As Detective Pratt stated, State Patrol is on their way to Eagle Pass. As we speak , they will be dealing with the Sheriff's arrest. They are giving us the pleasure of dealing with you." Sgt. Brocard smirked.

"All this over a brat?" Culpepper huffed.

Swede growled as Pratt and Brocard placed a hand on his arms to hold him back. "You didn't want to cooperate when we came here earlier when we were nice. We did our homework on you. Now, you have a choice, a really simple one actually." Pratt informed Culpepper.

"And pray tell, what are my choices, bitch?" Culpepper growled at the women.

"Aww, Detective, I think he's trying to offend us." Sgt. Brocard laughed. "Simple, your choices are you cooperate with us in every way with this investigation into Emma Patterson's disappearance or we can contact State Patrol and inform them of the outstanding warrant for your arrest."

"Or" Pratt said, looking over at her team leader, "we can inform Sandy Whitaker's father where Culpepper is and allow him to take out the trash. The trash being you

Culpepper, seeing as the man has been looking for you since you raped, sodomized and humiliated his fourteen-year-old daughter in front of a crowd." Pratt shrugged, looking at Culpepper, bopping her head from side to side.

"You're cops, you can't do shit like that. Besides, you have nothing. There is no warrant for my arrest and Whittaker has no proof I was the one who fucked his whore of a daughter." Culpepper spewed.

"As of 0900 hours yesterday morning, a warrant for your arrest was issued by San Diego PD for rape and first degree murder of both Sandy Whittaker and a Candance Pernell." Sgt. Brocard said, staring Culpepper down.

"The warrant is being served on your personal properties in San Diego, Miami, and Las Vegas. It's also being served on your father's personal properties in San Diego, Manhattan, and Aspen. It's only a matter of time before a warrant is served here as well. Now, we can either speed that arrest up by informing SDPD we've found you in the course of our investigation, *or* we can give you time to assist us in our investigation, putting in a good word for you with the DA.

It's up to you Culpepper." Pratt said firmly, continuing to look Culpepper in the eyes, not backing down.

"Bullshit. You're bluffing, there is no warrant." Culpepper yelled at Pratt, standing up to show his dominance against her.

"Sandy and Candance's bodies were found several days ago. Eyewitnesses put you as the last person to have seen them alive." Sgt Brocard informed Culpepper.

"Eyewitnesses? But no DNA evidence shows me with them. You have nothing, you stupid bitches."

"Hmmm we never said that. We are going to let SDPD and the DA have the fun of informing you of what evidence they have against you. Oh, and just to let you know, daddy has no more favors to call in to save you now."

"So, what's the decision, Culpepper? We arrest you now or later after you've helped us?" Pratt asked, twirling her handcuffs around on her index finger.

"Fucking bitches. What do you want to know?" Culpepper huffed.

"Who came on your property a few days ago in a tricked out truck with chains on the tires?" Sgt Brocard asked, straight to the point.

"I don't fucking know. I don't keep up with who drives what around here. These are men, not little boys who still need their daddy showing them how to piss."

"Strike one. You have two more chances Culpepper." Pratt said, clicking the cuffs.

"What are we playing now? Baseball? I definitely have the bat!" Culpepper said, smirking as he reached below the desk.

"First, hands on the desk where I can see them. Second, keep dreaming mister. Grabbing your crotch thinking that turns a woman on is why you're in the shitshow you're in now. I'm into real men, not boys who would turn a woman into a lesbian with one look at his micro penis." Pratt said, causing Sgt. Brocard, Highlander and Swede to cough, hiding their laugh.

"Bitch!" Culpepper growled.

"Again, with names, sheesh! Now, let's try it again. The truck?"

"I don't know! Several of my men drive fucking trucks. Some of them have lifts and some don't. The lifts handle the terrain better." Culpepper yelled.

"Strike two. Anyone with half a brain

knows that lifts do not make a truck safer or handle rocky terrains better. It makes them easier to tip over. Last chance Culpepper." Pratt said, stepping forward with the cuffs twirling on her fingertips.

"Look, I don't know what the hell you two want. Several of my seasonal guys have trucks with lifts. Since they are adults, they come and go as they please. I have no fucking control on what they do." Culpepper yelled out, standing up from behind his desk.

Sgt. Brocard and Pratt looked at each other then shrugged. "Jasper Culpepper, you're under arrest for the rape and murder of Sandy Whittaker and Candance Pernell..." Sgt. Brocard said as she walked around the desk.

Suddenly, Culpepper turned, striking out at Brocard with a closed fist, aiming for her face. Sgt. Brocard stepped back, using Culpepper's momentum against him, she grabbed his wrist and upper arm, swinging Culpepper around. As Sgt. Brocard swung him around, she dropped to her knee, forcing Culpepper to scream out in pain as he fell to the floor, face first.

Pratt ran to Sgt. Brocard, securing Culpepper's free hand, placing it behind his back into handcuffs. Sgt. Brocard then twisted the arm she had behind Culpepper's back and placed it into the cuffs, securing both arms, before standing up.

"You ok Sarge?" Pratt asked, looking Sgt. Brocard over.

"Yeah, saw his movement before he could connect. Safe to say he's never been a part of fight club." Sgt. Brocard said, laughing.

"He's apparently never learned to fight on his own, that's for sure. Damn ladies, if I wasn't already hitched..." Swede chuckled, as Highlander growled beside him.

"Yeah, yeah, whatever. Let's read this piece of shit his rights and take him in. He's fried now." Pratt said, wiping at her knees and hands.

Sgt. Brocard proceeded to re-read Culpepper his rights as she and Pratt pulled him to his feet. As they were getting Culpepper to his feet, several of his ranch employees came running into the office with weapons drawn. Both women looked at each other then over at the men who ran into the room. The two women drew their weapons at the same time Highlander and Swede drew theirs.

"I highly doubt you gentlemen, and I use

that term loosely right now, want to sit in a jail cell with this man." Sgt. Brocard calmly said, holding onto Culpepper's upper arm with her weapon in her dominate hand.

"Shoot these bitches right now! They assaulted me!" Culpepper screamed at his men.

"Riiight!" Pratt mocked. "Yet the cameras will show how you swung first and sarge here handed you your ass. Now, boys, you can holster your weapons and we'll walk out of here, no problems, or you can fire your weapons, take us out, then pray like hell the teams we have surrounding the property doesn't riddle your useless assess with bullets. For those of you that survive, then well, it'll be the electric chair. When your asses show up in hell, Satan himself will have those little French maid outfits and pineapples waiting for you."

"The fuck does dresses, and pineapples have to do with anything?" A ranch hand asked.

"Sheesh really? You guys are boring as hell. Basically, you shoot us, since Satan loves us with all the business we send his way, especially lately, we get to make bitches out of you in hell, shoving pineapples up your asses every day, for eternity." Pratt shrugged. "Your choice!"

Sgt. Brocard coughed a laugh as she saw Swede and Highlander cringe out of the corner of her eye. "I highly recommend putting your weapons away gentlemen. She would take too much pleasure in the pineapple scenario."

"Fucking useless, all of you. Mackey, call my father, have him get ahold of my damn attorney." Culpepper demanded.

"Hope the dude can practice here in Montana, otherwise you're screwed, not in the nice way either. I'm sure you'll make a nice little bitch in jail. Curious here Jasper, how's your head giving skills?" Pratt asked, taunting Culpepper as they walked him out of the house.

"Damn, they're hot when they work." Highlander murmured to Swede as his wife walked past him.

"Yeah, I have to agree, you're one lucky son of a bitch." Swede chuckled.

CHAPTER 14

Alpha Squad arrived back at the Patterson Ranch several hours after arresting Culpepper. They found Hank, Blakely, Collins, and Johns still going through files, discussing what Hank would remember from the file. Swede, Highlander, Mac, Doc and Snake walked into the room behind Alpha Squad, then headed over to the group and sat down.

"How did it go with Culpepper?" Hank asked without looking up.

"As we figured. Guy was arrogant as all get out. Brocard took him down when he swung at her. Yelled for them to call his father and lawyer. He's down at the jailhouse now. They interrogated his tail left and right, but he claims he knows nothing." Swede said with a chuckle, pointing at Sgt. Brocard over his shoulder.

"You believe him?" Blakely questioned, looking over at Swede.

"At this point, yes. Those gals rode him hard in their questions and he never budged. He's pissed as high hell his daddy hasn't called them off yet. How goes it here?"

Hank sighed, closing the folder he was looking at and leaned back as if stretching his back. "No damn where. Nothing we've looked at so far shows anything that would have them coming after me. Hell, we both know if any of these people came after us, they would have stuck out like a sore thumb."

Swede picked up a folder from the pile and opened it. "Hell, I remember this one. I thought the XO was going to have a cow when word came down that the attorney was fishing for the names of Gold Team."

Hank stood up and walked over towards Swede. "What are you talking about?"

"Remember that mother who was screaming that we killed her son when we went after that war lord, Abdul Sahalin, who was sympathetic with the Taliban and wanted them in power?"

"The one that was all over the news?"

"Yeah, that one. She claimed that her son was a decorated soldier who was helping protect innocent women and children along with other soldiers in the area that we hit. Screamed that SEALs murdered her son and other soldiers. But when XO investigated, no one knew what she was talking about."

"Shit what was his name?"

Swede and Hank went further over the notes until they found what they were looking for. "His name was Jason Mackey."

"Wait, did you say Mackey?" Raso asked, standing up, looking over at Pratt.

"Yeah, why?" Hank asked confused.

"Wait a damn minute, didn't Culpepper yell for a Mackey to call his sperm donor?" Pratt asked Swede and Highlander.

"Holy shit! What the hell was his name?" Swede said, his eyes getting big as he stared at Pratt.

"Bernard Mackey. One of the ones who didn't want to put away his gun. Kept looking at you funny. I thought he just swung to the left a little bit, if you know what I mean." Pratt said, wiggling her eyebrows at Swede.

"Really funny. But yeah, you're right, he did keep staring at me a little too hard." Swede said, looking at Hank.

"How common is the Mackey name?" Blakely asked the two men.

"Around here, it's not. Never heard of it until today at Culpepper's." Hank answered.

"I've heard his name around town some. He's an arrogant jackass who thinks he's God's gift to the women around town. Heard rumors he was trying to get into the pants of one of the locals while he was bagging a few others, but no one knew who it was."

"I'm going to fucking kill him!" Lone growled as he started to storm off before Wildcard could grab his arm.

"Hold on, spill it for the rest of us."

"The local he's trying to bag is my sister, Lisa. She's been seeing him for almost six months now. He's been at the house pretty much every single night almost. I hate his ass and my sister knows it. He knows I don't think too highly of his mug either."

"Wildcard, you hang out with Lone some, have you ever met this Bernard guy?" Hank asked Wildcard.

"Yeah, he's an arrogant jackass. I knew he wasn't being faithful to Lisa but no proof to say otherwise. She's head over heels for the guy."

"Well, we can say it's unanimous that no

one likes this twatscicle." Diesel chimed in.

"Have you ever had a real conversation with the guy?" Hank asked Lone.

"No, but Lisa made sure I knew all this deets so I didn't kill the guy for trying to get into her pants." Lone answered, growly.

"What has she told you about him?" Hank asked, looking at the folder in his hands.

"He came here about a year ago, hasn't been in town that long. Good friends with his boss, but she never mentioned who it was. The boss moved his mom here with him since he's an only child. That was about it." Lone said, looking around, trying to remember if he forgot anything.

"Has he ever mentioned a brother?" Swede asked.

"No, he doesn't really talk when I'm around. Pretty much stays quiet unless he and Lisa are talking. He knows I don't like him or trust him, so he pretty much doesn't hang out at the house for long when I get home."

"Where does his mother live? Do you know?" Sgt. Brocard asked Lone.

"If I remember correctly, I think Lisa said the mother lived on the property where he works, a bit away from the main house. Supposedly the boss has a small place near the edge of the property in the back." Lone mentioned, looking over at Wildcard.

"Well we now know that his 'boss' is none other than Culpepper. I think it's time we go have a meeting with Mackey and find out where Emma is. I say we split up, as much as I hate it." Sgt. Brocard said to the room full of people. "Blakely, are you able to assist us with this or are you limited?"

"What do you need Sargent?" Blakely asked, stepping forward.

"Hank, with your permission, this is your town, and your daughter, I suggest we split up. One team go deal with Mackey himself, and the other go to find his mother."

"What if we went as one, confronted Culpepper about the cabin and then split up, one tackle Mackey and the other his mother. Culpepper isn't able to get visitors or make phone calls right now, so he'd have no way of telling Mackey we're coming. State troopers have his tail now, so he can't buy anyone off inside the jailhouse." Rameriez suggested.

"Except that deputy who doesn't like us." York reminded everyone.

"We can warn the state troopers about him and they can deal with it." Pratt said, looking over at Hank. "Your call big guy."

"I know which deputy you're talking about. I'll deal with him personally. I agree, we need to talk to Culpepper about Mackey's mom. I say, the group that's going to go and talk to Culpepper and the other group go and talk to Mackey. Keep him occupied while we go after the mother. We've only got one shot at this. Let's get my daughter and bring her home."

"Hank, I know you want to be on the team that confronts the mother and find Emma." Pratt started. "Hold on now, hear me out. Let Swede be on that team, she will have her uncle, if she's there. I think if you're with us confronting Mackey, we have a better chance of getting him to slip up and incriminate himself in your daughter's disappearance. We'll get it out of him faster than if it was just Swede."

"She has a point brother. Granted we were both on that team, but he came after your daughter. Nail his ass to the wall. I'll find Emma and get her to you stat." Swede said, speaking low to Hank, agreeing with the women's assessments.

"Find my daughter and bring her home." Hank said, without hesitation. "Let's do this."

CHAPTER 15

THE TEAM SPLIT INTO TWO. "Ok, this is how the teams should go, I'll take Swede, Lone, Jones, Collins, Doc, Snake, York and Rameriez. Doc, I want you to go with us in case Emma is there at the house and needs medical attention. We don't know what kind of condition they've kept the place in or what they've done with her, if anything. The rest of you go with Hank. Hank, as hard as it will be for you, I need you to stand back with Blakely, Highlander, Mac and Wildcard. Let the women do their thing." Sgt. Brocard said, saying who should go where.

"Keep your coms on, we need to play it off like we're needing information on Culpepper. If we go in too strong, he'll clam up and it will take forever to get anything out of him. Even if Hank comes in with his alphaness." Pratt agreed, suggesting an approach.

"Alphaness? Is that even a word?" Blakely asked, shaking his head at Pratt with a smirk.

"As much as I hate having to stay back on all of this, I agree with Laura. I'll wait in the truck with the guys, you ladies do your thing."

"So, do we need a safe word or something?" Diesel asked, looking at the group she was assigned to.

"Safe word?" Collins asked confused.

"Duh, like pineapple or red?" Diesel asked, innocently causing several people to groan and lower their heads.

"I seriously worry about you sometimes! This isn't a BDSM club we're going into, you dork. It's a code word that we need to have the team running in." Raso said laughing at the rest of the group. "But she has a point. We need a word for the rest of the team waiting outside incase Mackey gets froggy."

"I think we should wait to go inside the property until Sarge talks to Culpepper about where the mother's place is. Once her team has confirmation on the cabin and are headed that way, then we go in and get Mackey talking. Once word has been confirmed that Emma is safe and sound, then Hank comes in and we take his ass down once and for wall." Pratt said, shrugging as she looked at everyone then lowered her head at the stares. "Or not. Either way."

"She's right, if we rush in too soon, who's to say they don't have something worked out to give each other a heads up when trouble is on the way. We know for a fact there was four people. Three who did the kidnapping and a driver. So, we need to be careful how we handle this until we have Emma in custody." Sgt. Brocard said, nodding at Pratt.

An hour later, a plan was hatched on how both teams would handle their parts. Swede and his group left for the jail house while Hank and his group left to sit near the Culpepper Ranch. They drove to Lone's ranch first to make sure that Mackey wasn't there visiting Lisa with the excuse that Lone had forgotten something in his room.

Once they were in place just off the property, out of site, they received the call from Lone that Culpepper sang like a canary about a cabin and gave up the location, confused why they were asking about a crazy old woman. The team was headed to the cabin now.

Raso, Cortez, Diesel and Pratt got into one vehicle to encounter Mackey first, while Hank, Blakely Highlander, Mac and Wildcard held back a bit to listen in. The four women got out of the car and went to the door and knocked. After informing the staff member they were here to speak with Mackey, they were led to Culpepper's office. Ten minutes after being led into the office, Mackey walked into the room.

"What the hell do you bitches want now? We're already in an uproar trying to get things dealt with thanks to you."

"Does Lisa know you like to call women bitches? Or is it just us?" Raso asked, turning around to face Mackey.

"What do I owe the pleasure." Mackey backtracked, with a glare.

Raso hid the cringe at the skeevy smile that Mackey gave her. "I'm here to gather more information on Culpepper. We think he was behind the kidnapping of Emma Patterson."

"The fuck would he want to kidnap that brat for?" Mackey fired back.

"Brat? Seriously? What is it with men and

the word brat? The *child* has a name." Pratt responded, walking over towards Mackey from the corner.

"Sorry, let me rephrase my question, what would my boss need the fucking brat for?"

"Oh, I don't know, collateral to get what he wanted? It's no secret that he's been begging for the Patterson land. His daddy got pissed when Hank turned him down flat and he was stuck buying this plot. Everyone knows Hank's lot is bigger and better than Culpepper's."

Mackey snorted a laugh. "For now. Culpepper is in negotiations with the ranches surrounding him to buy up theirs."

"And failing miserably. See, we've already talked to Frank, the guy who has the ranch behind you and the Watsons, the ranch to the east. Culpepper talked to them but they both turned him down flat. They have no desire to sell since their ranches have been in their families for generations. I know for a fact Culpepper tried to talk to the Logan's. I also know that Lone told him to get the hell off the property. Now if you're dating his sister to soften her up, then let me burst that bubble for you cowboy, she *can't* sell the property."

Mackey laughed again. "She can her portion of it."

Raso laughed outright, shaking her head. "Yeah Lone is right about you. You're a whole French fry meal short of a happy meal. Let me lay it out for you Mackey boy, his sister cannot and will not sell the property. You see, both of their names are on that deed and both must sign any paper for the sale to be legal. There is no portion to Lone nor is there just a portion for Lisa. It belongs to the both of them. Without both signatures, you don't get jack shit."

"Well I'm sure if something were to happen ..." Mackey said, eyes gleaming towards Raso.

"Did you just threaten my partner?" Pratt said, stepping forward before Diesel and Cortez could stop her.

"Just stating a fact." Mackey smirked.

"Then let me dispel you of that notion also, dumbass. Even if you were smart enough to kill Lone, you still wouldn't get the land. The land cannot change hands for ten years after his death. So, guess what, it still isn't going to Culpepper, even if he was smart enough to talk Lisa into marrying him, he couldn't do shit with the land without her signature, *and* that of their attorney." Cortez said, smirking back at Mackey.

"I'm curious if Lisa knows about all the other women you've been banging while you're with her?" Diesel popped up, walking into the room. "Sorry, I just saw one of his tarts leaving the house getting dressed.

"Considering there are about a hundred other men that stay here on this property, what the hell makes you think she was with me?" Mackey asked, sneering at Diesel.

"Umm, well she came out of your room and you're only one of six people besides Culpepper who stay in this house. Sorry, spoke to the housekeeper who kinda spilled the beans. You bad boy you." Diesel said, smirking.

"Yeah you'd make a horrible spouse, Mackey." Raso quipped.

"You came to say what you needed ladies, or was there more? Maybe you wanted to take your turn with me? See what the other women like to brag about?"

"Please don't make me puke. There's no way in hell I'd fuck you, even with a prosthetic pussy. And finally, what in the hell makes you think I'd even want to screw you? No, just no, hell no." Raso said, gagging.

"Everyone loves the Mac." Mackey bragged, grabbing his crotch.

"Yeah, I bet they don't come back for more. My take from the chick that left, she's regretting her five seconds with you, she hauled ass out of her and told the housekeeper to inform you to forget her number." Diesel said, laughing, and slapping her leg.

Just then, Hank, Blakely, Highlander, Mac and Wildcard walked into the room. Highlander walked over towards Pratt, while Hank and Blakely walked towards Mackey. Everyone noticed Mackey pale when Hank walked into the room.

"What the hell is this? What the fuck are you doing here Patterson?"

CHAPTER 16

RASO AND PRATT FLANKED HANK, offering silent support as Blakely, Highlander, and Mac hovered nearby in case they were needed. "Why? That's all I want to know, why?" Hank asked, seething.

"What in the hell are you talking about?" Mackey asked, confused.

"Well let's see, there's the kidnapping of Emma, his daughter. And there's the death of three Navy SEALs that he served with. I think he's asking why you felt the need to do all that?" Diesel answered for the room.

"SEALs? Dead? What the hell are you talking about? I haven't killed anyone." Mackey shrilled, backing away from Hank.

"What he's referring to, is three SEALs, still active duty were killed while on US soil. Then, oh wait, baby Emma goes missing." Pratt said, sarcastically.

"I know nothing about any SEALs dying. I have nothing to do with that. You can't pin that shit on me. I can prove I've been right here on this property. Or at the Logan's bagging that sweet snatch."

"No one said you did it personally. But you had a hand in it, like, maybe hiring someone." Raso sneered her despise.

"You really are stupid. Lone's sister will enjoy hearing you claim you 'bagged' her. Especially when she finds out it's because you thought you'd be able to take the land from under Lone's nose." Pratt mocked, stepping forward.

"Oh baby, if you stick around when the party leaves, I'm sure I can bag you too." Mackey winked at Pratt, causing Highlander to growl and step forward, while the other's stepped back slightly to give him room.

"Fucker is really stupid if he thinks Highlander won't kick his ass." Diesel murmured.

"Ok, you've claimed you had nothing to do with the SEALs, we'll come back to that, you didn't deny anything with Emma. Now talk. Where's Emma? Why did you take her?" Pratt demanded, walking towards Mackey.

"Do you see or hear a brat crying in here?" Mackey mocked back at the group.

"Call my kid a brat one more time!" Hank growled as he stepped forward.

"You think you're so big and bad, don't you? All you SEALs think you're untouchable. You couldn't even have the common decency to apologize to my mother or me for killing my brother. She couldn't even sue your asses for his death. You fuckers were protected by the fucking government." Mackey screamed out.

"So, you kidnapped an innocent child?" Pratt asked, ready to beat Mackey.

"I had to get his attention. He and his men took my brother, so I took his daughter. He's lucky I didn't have my men take out his wife in the process. Eye for an eye really." Mackey laughed.

"You seriously have a death wish dumbass." Diesel mumbled outloud.

"My brother was a loyal soldier for the US Army. He didn't deserve to die with his brothers in arms by his own country. You were on the same fucking side."

"Your brother wasn't in Afghanistan as a

US Soldier, Mackey. He left the Army after four years and then joined a security company that did work overseas for rich men. He went to work for a company called Grey Securities. He was over there working security for a war lord by the name of Ali Rejeniah Mohamad. Mohamad was a Taliban supporter, drug lord and a human trafficker of young woman in his country." Blakely informed Mackey of his dead brother.

"You lie!" Mackey screamed, taking a step towards Blakely.

"No, he's not." Pratt said, bracing to intervene. "We called Grey Securities, they've been under investigation for years because of the type of work they accept. They started doing the work they did when they lost all their government contracts after one of their operatives got busted for drug running and killing a kid overseas. They started working for drug lords, protecting the Taliban instead. They moved their offices out of the US and into Dubai. That is where your brother was based out of."

"When we were dispatched to Afghanistan, we were ordered to take out the war lord, *because* he was targeting US soldiers. He was giving money to the Taliban to torture soldiers they captured. We saw your brother and a few other Americans, tried to get them out, warned them they needed to get out before the charges went off, but they wouldn't leave. They opened fire on us. We defended ourselves. End of story." Hank recalled.

"You're lying. My brother wrote my mother every week. He sent her money to pay all her bills. No way he would dishonor our family by doing what you're claiming." Mackey cried out.

"Think about it, Mackey, on a soldier's salary, even his rank, what he did in the military, even with the extra pay from being overseas, he wouldn't have made enough to take care of his bills and your mother's too. Grey Securities paid her nearly a quarter of a million dollars in life insurance when he died in Afghanistan, paid off all his bills as well as hers, per his request. Grey Securities even paid for his funeral. The military wouldn't have done that." Hank informing, Mackey how the military works. "Had he still been an active duty soldier, two uniformed soldiers would have showed up at your mother's door.

They would have paid for the trip from where his body was to his hometown and the funeral, but that would have been it. Your mother would have gotten a folded flag and *only* his life insurance policy. That is all that would have happened.

"Taking my daughter won't bring your brother back. He made his choice, we tried to get him to leave but he wouldn't. Nothing we could have done." Hank finished up.

"But Bishop said they were still active duty when you murdered my brother..." Mackey whispered loudly.

"Bishop Monroe?" Blakely asked, looking over at Pratt.

"Are you fucking kidding me? You're taking the word of Bishop Monroe?" Pratt asked, shocked.

"He served with my brother." Mackey explained.

"No, he didn't" Blakely answered. "Monroe was dishonorably discharged after two years in the Marine Corps when he raped a girl in Afghanistan. Grey Securities took him on when they moved to Dubai, just before they hired your brother." Pratt said, shaking her head. "The fool has been wanted by San Diego PD for years, but he's been overseas, we couldn't touch him as long as he's there."

"He's here in Montana working for Culpepper after all the surgeries he had to have due to the injuries he sustained in Afghanistan. He was with my brother when he was killed. He was the one who told momma that they were still active duty and that it was the SEALs who killed him." Mackey confessed.

"Wasn't Grey Securities shut down recently?" Raso asked Blakely.

"Yeah, some of their operatives were busted helping ISIS last year, when they were under investigation, their response was money talked so they went with whoever paid the most money. Dubai police arrested them, kicked them out of the country and the brothers are serving a fifteen-year prison sentence."

"Ok, so if Mackey is telling the truth, what if it was Monroe who was killing the SEALs? He is a former Marine Recon, served time in Afghanistan and knows how the SEALs operate." Pratt suggested.

"Collins just sent a text, Emma is safe.

They took out several guards around the cabin, one has been confirmed as Bishop Monroe. Guess we got justice for the SEALs without even realizing it. Oh, and Mackey, your mother confessed to everything." Blakely informed the whole room.

"Bernard Mackey, you're under arrest for the kidnapping of Emma Patterson..." Diesel said as she handcuffed him and lead him out of the room.

Hank slowly walked out of the house processing all that he'd learned in the last thirty minutes. So much hate in one person for the wrong reasons. Lies that cost innocent people their lives. Good SEALs who served their country with honor, his brothers in blood, sweat and tears, gone, because of a man's greed. His daughter kidnapped and held by strangers, because of a man's need for vengeance due to greed. A good man driven to commit crimes because of his brother's refusal to admit he was working for the wrong side.

As soon as Hank stepped outside, he heard the sweetest sound, his daughter's squeal of 'daddy'. When Hank looked over at his brother-in-law, Emma was trying to get out of Swede's arms, reaching for him. Hank quickly walked over to Swede, pulling Emma into his arms, holding her tightly, inhaling her sweet baby scent.

Alpha Squad stood together, along with Blakely, Agent Collins, Agent Johns, Highlander, Doc, Snake and Mac. The women all stood there with huge smiles on their faces and watched the scene before them.

"That's the most beautiful scene a person can witness." Raso stated.

"Aye, someday ye will have ye own to hold and cherish. If ye would stop being so damn stubborn." Highlander stated.

"Keep dreaming asshole. Your brother has plenty of other offers he can choose from. Red, get control of your man before I hurt him" Raso quipped as she walked away.

"Babe, stop picking on her. The more we keep pushing, the further she will move away from him. They have to move at their own speed."

"I know lass. Just hate the hurt in his eyes. She doesn't see it."

"Give it time handsome. She's still healing from pain she's refused to let go. Until she heals from that, she can't move forward. They will get there. Now, let's get home to our own bundles of joy." Pratt said, kissing her husband and heading off to their waiting SUV.

THE END

ORIGINAL BROTHERHOOD
PROTECTORS SERIES

BY ELLE JAMES

ABOUT ELLE JAMES

ELLE JAMES also writing as MYLA JACKSON is a *New York Times* and *USA Today* Bestselling author of books including cowboys, intrigues and paranormal adventures that keep her readers on the edges of their seats. With over eighty works in a variety of sub-genres and lengths she has published with Harlequin, Samhain, Ellora's Cave, Kensington, Cleis Press, and Avon. When she's not at her computer, she's traveling, snow skiing, boating, or riding her ATV, dreaming up new stories. Learn more about Elle James at www.ellejames.com

Website | Facebook | Twitter | GoodReads | Newsletter | BookBub | Amazon

Follow Elle!
www.ellejames.com
ellejames@ellejames.com

facebook.com/ellejamesauthor

twitter.com/ElleJamesAuthor